S

"Antonio, a girl has her pride."

"Pride?"

"Everyone knows you're the love-'em-and-leave-'em type. I have no intention of being added to your list of idle conquests. So you can lend me the money for a taxi."

Antonio began to fume. *We'll see about that, Miss Love-'em-and-leave-'em yourself! I've got news for you. You won't be loving and leaving me, honey. You're going to be my wife.* "I wouldn't dream of sending you home in a taxi," he said with a smooth smile. "Just give me a minute...."

Miranda Lee

THE BLACKMAILED BRIDEGROOM

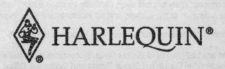

HARLEQUIN®

TORONTO • NEW YORK • LONDON
AMSTERDAM • PARIS • SYDNEY • HAMBURG
STOCKHOLM • ATHENS • TOKYO • MILAN • MADRID
PRAGUE • WARSAW • BUDAPEST • AUCKLAND

ISBN 0-373-12151-2

THE BLACKMAILED BRIDEGROOM

First North American Publication 2001.

Copyright © 1999 by Miranda Lee.

Visit us at www.eHarlequin.com

Printed in U.S.A.

CHAPTER ONE

THE jumbo jet was twenty minutes late setting down at Mascot Airport, but Antonio was one of the first to alight. The head of Fortune Productions, European Division, didn't look as if he'd been on a gruelling twenty-two-hour flight from London to Sydney. His superb grey suit was sleek and uncrumpled. His thick jet-black hair was slicked back from a freshly shaven face. His dark eyes were clear and rested.

The advantage of flying first class.

Not that Antonio Scarlatti had always travelled first class. He knew what it was like to do it tough. He knew what it was like to travel long hauls cramped in steerage, with wall-to-wall passengers and little chance of sleep, then have people look down their nose at him at the other end, when his suit had been wrinkled and his job far less prestigious than the one he now held.

Antonio had no intention of ever going back to that existence. He'd made it to the top, and the top was where he was going to stay. The world was for the winners. And the wealthy. At the age of thirty-four, he was finally both.

The company limousine was waiting in its usual spot, the engine idling at the ready. Antonio opened the back door and slid into its air-conditioned comfort.

'Morning, Jim,' he addressed the chauffeur.

'Mornin', Tone.'

Antonio smiled. He was back in Australia all right. In London, and all over Europe, he was always addressed by his drivers as 'Mr Scarlatti'. But that wasn't the way down under, especially after an acquaintance of some time.

Antonio leant back against the plush leather seat with a deeply relaxing sigh. It was good to be home and off the merry-go-round for a fortnight's break. His contract stated he could fly home for two weeks rest and recuperation every three months, a necessity since he worked seven days a week when on the job. Being in charge of selling and promoting Fortune Productions' extensive list of television programmes to the hundreds of stations and cable networks all over Europe was a challenging job.

'Straight home, Jim,' he said, and closed his eyes. He'd bought himself a luxury serviced apartment overlooking the harbour bridge a couple of years back, and couldn't wait to immerse himself in its privacy and comfort. The last few days had been a nightmare of negotiations and never-ending meetings. Antonio needed some peace and quiet.

'No can do, Tone,' the chauffeur returned as he eased the lengthy car past the long line of taxis which had queued up to meet the flight from London. 'The boss wants you to join him for breakfast.'

Antonio's eyes opened on a low groan. He hoped it wasn't one of those media circus breakfasts Conrad was always getting invited to and which he occasionally attended. Antonio couldn't stand them at the best of times. 'Where, for pity's sake?' came his irritable query.

'The Taj Mahal.'

'Thank God,' Antonio muttered.

The Taj Mahal was Jim's nickname for Conrad Fortune's residence at Darling Point. It was an apt term. The place was over the top with its grandeur and opulence, a monolithic mansion sprawled across an acre of some of the most expensive land in Sydney's exclusive Eastern suburbs.

What the house lacked in taste, it made up for in sheer size. The façade had more columns than the Colosseum, the foyer more marble than the British Museum, and Romanesque statues and ornate fountains dominated the front landscaping. The sloping backyard was more low key, terraced to incorporate the solar-heated swimming pool and two rebound ace tennis courts.

Antonio thought the place ostentatious in the extreme. But it *was* impressive, no doubt about that. Socialites grovelled to be included on the lists for Conrad's celebrated parties. Magazines and television programmes clamoured to photograph beyond the high-security walls which enclosed the property.

Not Conrad's television programmes, of course. They knew better.

'You wouldn't have any idea what he wants me for, Jim, would you?' Antonio probed.

'Nope.' A man of few words, Jim.

Antonio decided not to speculate. Time would tell, he supposed.

Fifteen minutes later, the limousine slid to a smooth halt in front of the grand front steps, and this time Jim did the honours with the door.

'You won't be needing that,' he advised when Antonio went to pick up his laptop.

Antonio shot the chauffeur a sharp look. So he *did* have some idea of what was up. And clearly it wasn't a business matter.

Curiouser and curiouser.

The housekeeper answered the door. Evelyn was in her late forties, and very homely, as were all of Conrad's female employees. No fool, was Conrad. He'd been stung once, by an ambitious and beautiful maid, and had no intention of harbouring any females under his roof who might present him with unwise temptations. Although now rising seventy, Conrad was still very interested in the opposite sex, as evidenced by the three mistresses he kept. One here in Sydney, one in Paris and one in the Bahamas.

Evelyn had been Conrad's housekeeper now for over a decade. She was efficient and reliable. More importantly, she knew how to keep her mouth shut to the press.

'Conrad's expecting you,' she told Antonio straight away. 'He's in the morning room.'

The morning room overlooked the terrace, which overlooked the pool. The floor-to-ceiling windows faced north-east, and captured the sun all year round. On a winter morning, the room was a dream. In summer, the air-conditioning had a tough job preventing the place from turning into a hothouse. Spring found it coolish, especially since the sun was only just rising at six-thirty.

Conrad was sitting at the huge glass oval table in the centre of the conservatory-style room, wrapped in a thick navy bathrobe. Despite his age, he still had a full head of hair—a magnificent silvery grey—and piercing blue eyes. They flicked up at Antonio's entrance, and raked him from head to toe, disconcerting Antonio for a moment. Why on earth was Conrad looking him over like that, as though he'd come to audition for one of his soap operas? What was going on here?

'Sit down, Antonio,' Conrad ordered. 'Take a load off your feet and have some decent coffee for a change.' He picked up the coffee pot and poured an extra mugful of steaming brown liquid.

'What's the problem?' Antonio asked as he sat down and pulled the coffee towards him.

His employer gave him another long, considering look over the table, and Antonio's gut tightened further. He knew, without being told, that he wasn't going to like what Conrad had to say.

'Paige has come home again,' came the abrupt announcement.

Antonio almost said, So? What's new?

Conrad's wild and wilful daughter had been running away from home regularly since she was seventeen. She turned up again regularly too, every year or so. But no sooner had she returned than she'd be off again, saying she was going to share a flat with some girlfriends. But only once had this been the case. Usually, when the private investigator's report came in several weeks later, her flatmate was male and good-looking, invariably an artist or a musician. Paige seemed to like creativeness. Not one of them had denied sharing more with Paige than the cooking.

At first, Conrad had worried Paige might be exploited for her money. A whole family could have lived comfortably on his only child's generous monthly allowance! But perversely, from the day she'd first left home, Paige had never touched a cent of the thousands deposited in her bank account every month. When Conrad had found out his money was being donated to the RSPCA, and that Paige was working to support herself, he'd stopped the allowance altogether.

'Let her work, if that's what she wants to do!' he'd raged to Antonio, but would still cringe when he learnt that she was working as a waitress in some café, or behind the bar in a club or pub.

His worst nightmare, however, was that Paige would

fall pregnant to one of her live-in boyfriends and then bring the baby home with her. Conrad was not large on babies. Which gave Antonio an idea.

'She's not pregnant, is she?' he asked.

'No, but she's going to come to a sticky end, that girl, unless I do something about it. Do you realise she turns twenty-three next week?'

Antonio was surprised. How the years had flown!

'I would imagine you've tried everything,' he said sincerely. Most girls would give their eye-teeth for what Paige had once had. A lovely home. Designer clothes. An allowance fit for a princess, if she'd wanted to claim it. If none of that was enough to keep her happy, and at home, then Lord knows what was!

'Not…everything,' Conrad said slowly, and he set those penetrating blue eyes on Antonio again. 'There's one thing I haven't tried.'

'And what's that?'

'Marriage,' he pronounced. 'To a man who could control her.'

Antonio couldn't help it. He laughed. 'You think Paige would marry a man of your choice?'

'Of course not. I was thinking of a man of *her* choice. Namely, you, Antonio.'

'*Me?*' Antonio was floored.

'Yes, you. Don't pretend, Antonio. I know exactly what happened just before Paige ran away from home that first time. The first thing Lew did when I put him on the job of tracing her was to question all the staff here at Fortune Hall. Did you think that little incident by the pool between you and my daughter hadn't been overheard?'

When Antonio opened his mouth to explain, Conrad waved it shut.

'Please don't bother to defend your actions,' he swept on. 'You have nothing to answer for. You did exactly the right thing. How were you to know that the silly little fool would take your rejection so badly and run off with her broken heart?'

'Her heart wasn't broken,' Antonio contested heatedly. 'She took up with the next fellow soon enough!'

'A girl rarely forgets her first love.'

'I was *never* her love, first or otherwise!'

Hell, he hadn't even kissed the girl. He'd been polite to her when she'd been at home on holiday from boarding school, making small talk when their paths had crossed. Hard not to run into her when he'd been living at Fortune Hall in his position as Conrad's personal assistant, his first job with the company. No one had been more surprised than him when she'd thrown herself into his arms that day by the pool and declared her undying love and devotion.

Antonio hadn't taken advantage of her schoolgirl crush, despite acknowledging she was a serious temptation to any man, especially dressed as she'd been that day, in a minute pink bikini. On top of that, Antonio was always physically attracted to blond women. He especially liked tall, slender blond women, with big blue eyes, high, full breasts and a waist his hands could span.

His hands had spanned Paige's waist that day, as he'd reluctantly put her aside, then told her in no uncertain terms that he didn't return her feelings and that he thought of her as a silly little girl.

Not strictly true, of course. He'd thought of her as a silly *big* girl, extremely beautiful and extraordinarily sexy. Some evenings, when she'd been home from school and she'd come down to dinner in one of those tight, short low-cut little dresses she'd favoured, he'd been glad to be sitting at a table with a serviette covering his lap. If Paige had been any other man's daughter things might have turned out differently by the pool that day. But Antonio had had no intention of losing a second job because of the boss's daughter. No way!

Perhaps his rejection *had* been a little rough. Paige's obvious humiliation and tears had caused him pangs of guilt for a while, especially when she'd run away instead of returning to school, not sitting for her final exams into the bargain.

He'd got over his guilt soon enough, however, when Lew, Conrad's personal private investigator, had found her less than a month later, living on a remote North Coast beach with some surfing bum a good few years older than herself. Since the shack they'd been sharing only had one bedroom, it wasn't difficult to conclude their relationship had been far from platonic. She certainly hadn't denied it when Antonio himself had travelled all the way up there and tried to bring her back at Conrad's request.

Antonio's male ego had been dented by her indifferent reaction to his arrival on her doorstep, but any lingering concern for the girl had been well and truly dispelled once he'd seen for himself what sort of life she'd chosen to live.

Paige was trouble, in his opinion, an opinion reinforced every time their paths crossed, which thankfully wasn't often. The last time he'd seen her had been at Conrad's Christmas party the previous year. She'd sashayed downstairs, wearing a short strapless red dress which might have ended up around a less shapely females' ankles, so precariously had it been perched. To his eternal irritation and frustration, Antonio had found himself wanting to sweep her back up the stairs, rip that infernal scrap of red satin from her body and ravage her senseless upon the first available bed. Or floor. Or whatever.

Instead, he'd had to forcibly keep his eyes away from Paige's luscious young flesh, pretending to be enraptured by his date, a female lawyer on Fortune Productions' payroll. To his discredit, Antonio had shamelessly used the woman—both at the party and later—to sate the dark desires Paige had evoked.

Not that she'd minded. As it had turned out, she'd liked her sex a little rough, and without strings.

He hadn't seen Paige since that night, and tried not to think of her at all these days. But he was certainly thinking of her now.

'You can't be serious about this, Conrad,' he said disbelievingly.

'I'm very serious.'

'It's a crazy idea!'

'Why? She *was* in love with you once, whether you like it or not. And that was before you developed into the man you are today. Do you think I haven't noticed the way women react to you? You could make any woman fall in love with you. A girl like Paige should be a cinch.'

'But I don't *want* Paige to fall in love with me,' he pointed out icily. 'And I don't want to marry her.' Her, least of all, he thought angrily.

'Why?'

Antonio did not feel like explaining that he'd been in love very deeply once, with the daughter of his previous boss. He'd thought Lauren had loved him as much as he'd loved her. But when push had come to shove she hadn't been prepared to actually marry an Italian migrant with a questionable background and nothing to his name but his modest salary as a wine salesman. She'd just been slumming for a while, before moving on from her cosy, cushy life as a rich man's daughter to the cosy, cushy life of a rich's man's wife.

He'd stupidly turned up at her house on the night of her engagement party and made a big scene. Naturally, he'd been given the sack, with no references. It had been several months before he'd been able to get another job, during which he'd practically had to eat the paint off the walls. When Conrad had hired him to be his assistant and interpreter he'd been eternally grateful, even though he suspected he'd been the only applicant who could speak the five languages Conrad required during his business trips overseas.

Antonio had worked his guts out to get where he was today. He had no intention of giving it up for anyone, or of sharing his life with the same sort of silly, selfish, shallow creature who'd once almost destroyed him.

'When and if I marry, Conrad,' he said with cold fury, 'it will be because I'm so much in love that I couldn't bear not to.' Which was about as likely as Conrad himself breasting the altar once more.

When his boss said nothing to this, Antonio's black eyes narrowed. 'If I don't agree with this plan of yours, is it going to cost me my job?'

'No, of course not!' Conrad denied expansively. 'What kind of man do you take me for?'

Antonio hesitated to say. But you didn't get to be one of the richest men in Australia by being full of the milk of human kindness. Over the six years in Conrad's employ, Antonio had gleaned a lot of information about his boss.

Conrad had started out with nothing, as the son of penniless Polish migrants, changing his name from

Fortuneski to Fortune and getting in on the ground floor with television in Australia when it had started, in the fifties, working behind the camera at first before forming his own production company and buying the Australian rights to a successful American game show. It had made him his first million. More game shows had followed, and more millions. Then, in the late sixties, he'd tried one of the first soaps made in Australia, an outrageously sexy series which had made its name with scandalous storylines. Serious millions had begun to roll in, and Fortune Productions had never looked back. Neither had its ambitious bachelor owner.

Conrad had lived and breathed his work, and had had no intention of getting married. But then, in his mid-forties, Conrad had made the mistake of giving his then housekeeper *carte blanche* to hire and fire staff, and she'd taken on Paige's mother to serve at table. During a misguided interlude after a rather lengthy and boozy dinner party, Paige had been conceived.

Once presented with the reality of a child-to-be, Conrad had done the right thing and married the woman. He'd been hoping for a son and heir to take over the business. Instead, Paige had been born.

It had not been a happy union, and when his wife of one year had run off to America with a salesman, Conrad hadn't been shattered. Antonio imagined that his boss also hadn't lost much sleep over the news, a few years later, that his errant wife had been found dead in a New York hotel room of a drug overdose.

He was not a sentimental man.

'I'm planning on retiring at the end of the year,' Conrad went on now, snapping Antonio back to the matter at hand. 'I'll be moving permanently to my home in the Bahamas. When I do, the position of CEO of Fortune

Productions will become vacant. I intend to promote you, Antonio,' he said, and Antonio sucked in a sharp breath. 'But only if you're my son-in-law at the time,' Conrad finished.

Antonio exhaled with a rush. 'Damn and blast it, Conrad, that's blackmail!'

'No. That's good business. Who better to look after one's interests but family? You, as a born and bred Italian, should appreciate that.'

Antonio kept his temper with difficulty. 'And if I refuse?' he bit out.

'I'll make the same offer to Brock Masters. I imagine he could handle both jobs almost as well.'

Antonio gritted his teeth. Brock Masters was head of the North American Division. Publicly, he was all capped teeth and false charm, in Antonio's opinion. Handsome as Satan, but privately he had the morals of the Marquis de Sade.

'He'll ruin the company,' Antonio warned. 'And he'll destroy your daughter,' he added as an afterthought.

'If you think that, Antonio,' Conrad said smoothly, 'you know what to do.'

'You're a ruthless devil, do you know that?'

'Takes one to know one.'

'Yet you want me to marry your daughter!'

'She needs a real man for a change. One who will keep her on her toes in order to keep him. And one who can give her what she keeps looking for.'

'Which is?'

'What all women want. Love, of course.'

'For pity's sake, Conrad, you know darned well I don't love her.'

Conrad shrugged. 'What's love but an illusion anyway? Just tell Paige you love her. The silly little fool won't know the difference, as long as the sex is good. And the sex *will* be good, I'm sure. The way the ladies chase after you—even after one short evening in your bed—speaks volumes for your abilities in that department.'

Antonio stared at the man. He almost felt sorry for Paige, having such a cold-blooded bastard for a parent. He could not understand how a father could do such a thing to his daughter.

Still, Antonio was not a fool. He knew if he knocked Conrad back on this he was finished at Fortune Productions. Brock Masters hated his guts. Antonio supposed he could quit and find another job with a rival company, settle back and watch the rot set in at Fortune Productions. It would serve Conrad right if he did just that.

But pride in a job well done—and in the company—would not let him seriously consider such an action. And then there was the added image of Paige, being seduced, corrupted and destroyed by an amoral, cocaine-snorting pervert.

Antonio's stomach turned over. A silly little fool she might be, but she didn't deserve that.

'Under the circumstances,' he said, in that coolly ruthless voice which emerged when he was cornered, 'I will expect something in writing.'

Conrad beamed. 'But of course, Antonio. I'll have it ready for you when you come to dinner here tonight.'

Antonio frowned. 'Tonight?'

'I thought the sooner you got started the better. After all, you have to be back in London in a fortnight. A whirlwind romance is just what the doctor ordered. I see no reason why Paige shouldn't travel back with you, once she's wearing your engagement ring.'

'You expect her to agree to marry me in two short weeks?'

'You've negotiated more difficult contracts in much faster time, Antonio. Speaking of contracts, the day you marry Paige you will have your contract as CEO of Fortune Productions, plus I will give you the deeds to this house as a wedding present.'

'No, thank you, Conrad. The contract will do. I wouldn't want to live here.' Even if he could tolerate the space, he didn't want to be surrounded by Conrad's extra ears.

Conrad smiled. 'I had a feeling you'd say that. Shall we expect you around seven-thirty, then?'

'Are you sure Paige will still be here?' Antonio commented caustically.

'I should think so. Her latest boyfriend gave her quite a scare.'

'Oh?'

'He hit her.'

Antonio was surprised at how angry this news made him. There again, violence against women had always pushed savage buttons in him. 'I gather you know this charmer's name and address?' he ground out.

'Actually, no, I don't.'

'But you *always* know where Paige is living and who with!'

Conrad sighed. 'I stopped putting Lew on the job this past year. I just couldn't take it any more. I have no idea what she's been up to since January. Paige rang me out of the blue last night around one, and asked if Jim could come and pick her up at Central Station. She sounded scared, which, as you know, isn't like Paige at all. But the penny dropped once I saw the big bruise on her face.

She wouldn't tell me anything when I asked her last night. But maybe she'll tell you.'

'Maybe.' If she did, Antonio was going to teach the creep a lesson he wouldn't forget in a hurry!

Still, it had only been a question of time before Paige became mixed up with a really unsavoury type. The girl never could see the risks she was taking in living with men she didn't really know. She had no common sense, and no appreciation of the consequences of her actions. She'd be the perfect victim for the likes of Brock Masters!

Possibly there were excuses for her many and potentially dangerous relationships—Antonio was beginning to appreciate there'd been little enough warmth and affection here at home—but one would have thought she'd have learned by now. Almost twenty-three, and she was still looking for love in all the wrong places!

Well, she certainly won't find it with you, either, came the coldly cynical thought.

'You know, Conrad,' he said with a sardonic twist of his mouth. 'Has it occurred to you that Paige might say no to marriage, whether she falls in love with me or not?'

'It did cross my mind. If needs be, I suggest you use a method as old as time.'

'And what's that?'

'Get her pregnant.'

Antonio's eyes widened.

'I'm sure you won't find such a task beyond you,' his boss drawled. 'I gather the Wilding girl had to have a little operation before she could become engaged to the Jansen millions. Which was understandable. She couldn't risk a black-eyed baby born to a blond, blue-eyed father, could she?'

Antonio momentarily went white. Lauren had been *pregnant* when she'd run home to Daddy? She'd aborted *his* child, just to marry money?

'You really know how to strike below the belt, Conrad,' he said bitterly. 'How long have you known about my relationship with Lauren?'

'From the start. Do you honestly think I would employ a man to be my personal assistant and to live in my home if I hadn't had him thoroughly checked out? Forget the Wilding girl, Antonio. She was a fool, and so was her father. I know a good man when I see one. Marry my daughter, and you'll never regret it.'

Now *that*, Antonio conceded ruefully, was a matter of opinion.

Rising from his chair, he set a cool black gaze upon his future father-in-law and stretched out his hand. 'It's a deal.'

Conrad took, then pumped his hand. 'Splendid, my boy. Splendid. I knew you'd make the right decision. See you tonight, around seven-thirty. We'll have a celebratory drink together before dinner.'

Antonio said nothing to that, just spun on his heels and strode towards the doorway.

Evelyn barely had time to retreat hastily from where she'd been listening to every single word.

CHAPTER TWO

PAIGE woke mid-afternoon and just lay there for a while, staring up at the bedroom ceiling, thinking.

Home again.

If you could call this wretched house a home, that was.

The word *home* normally conjured up feelings of peace and warmth. It was where you could be yourself; where you were most relaxed; where you felt loved and accepted.

But home had never been like that for Paige. Fortune Hall was a cold, heartless place which evoked nothing in her but feelings of failure and inadequacy, of being unwanted and unloved, of being unsure of who she was or what she wanted out of life.

Only once had Paige momentarily been happy in this house: the year when Antonio Scarlatti had first come to Fortune Hall to live.

The memory of their first meeting was indelibly imprinted on her brain. It had been her last year in high school, and she'd caught the train home for the Easter break, feeling miserable when her father had said he couldn't possibly meet her at Central.

'Just catch a taxi home, Paige,' had been his offhand and impatient words on the telephone the night before. 'It's not as though it's far. I can't leave an important meeting for such a silly little thing.'

Such a silly little thing! That was what she was to him. A silly little thing. It was what she'd always been to him. A nuisance. An inconvenience. He'd never loved her, or made time for her. Not once.

Paige had stepped off the train at Central, no longer expecting to be met, so she'd been startled when a dark-haired, dashingly handsome young man had approached her and introduced himself as her father's new personal assistant, Antonio Scarlatti. She vaguely remembered thinking he didn't have an Italian accent at all, but that he had the most riveting eyes. Black and penetrating and incredibly sexy.

'Your father mentioned your arrival by train today,' he'd added, while those eyes held hers. 'I didn't think it right for you to make your way home all by yourself, so I told him it would be my pleasure to meet you. Come...' And he'd cupped her elbow with a gallant hand.

She'd been captivated from that moment.

Captivated and completely infatuated.

By the time he'd driven her through the gates of Fortune Hall, her racing heart had succumbed to a hero worship which had banished every other male idol whom her love-starved teenage heart had gathered over the previous few years. Her favourite music and movie stars were nothing compared to Antonio Scarlatti.

By the end of the two-week break she'd centred a thousand romantic hopes and dreams around him, crying her devastation when the holiday had ended all too swiftly. During the next term at school she'd spent long hours every day, imagining and fantasising all sorts of exciting scenarios with her handsome Italian at centre stage, till she'd begun to believe her own fantasies, turning each simple smile he'd given her into evidence that he was as secretly enamoured with her as she was with him.

Her schoolwork had suffered for her daydreaming,

and the comments on her report card had been none too impressive to bring home at the end of term: *Paige would do a lot better if only she would concentrate! Paige is an intelligent girl but her mind doesn't seem to be on her work!*

Which it hadn't been. Yet what a wonderful term it had been! What secret pleasures she'd hugged to herself, thinking about her beautiful Antonio all the time, weaving all sorts of fanciful dreams around him.

Her next holiday at home had seemed to cement all those dreams. The things he carefully hadn't said. Those secretive but scorching glances he'd bestowed on her across the dinner table. The way he'd held her slightly longer than necessary the day they'd run into each other on the stairs. The inordinate time he'd taken to help her find a book in the library one evening.

Paige had been sure he was just waiting till she finished school that year before he showed his hand. By then she would be eighteen, and a woman!

In her mind, they would eventually get married and have half a dozen babies, beautiful, black-eyed children who adored their mother and father and were so very happy, wrapped in the type of warm cocoon of family love that she'd never experienced herself, but she'd vowed to give *her* children.

By the time she'd come home again in September she'd become totally obsessed with him, her rather romantic feelings taking a more physical turn when she'd spotted him swimming in the pool the first morning of her holiday. She'd watched him from her bedroom window while he'd done lap after impressive lap, her eyes widening when he'd climbed out and just stood there as he towelled himself down, wearing only the briefest of black swimming costumes.

There had been something decidedly animal in his powerful physique, with its deeply olive skin and light covering of dark body hair, plus the way he was drying himself, with rough, rubbing strokes. Paige had gobbled him up with her eyes while the sexuality simmering deep within her feelings surfaced, stark and startling in its raw and naked need. Suddenly, she'd craved more than his love. She'd craved the man, and that part of him which made him a man, her galloping heart seizing up with shock at the explicitness of her desire.

When he'd looked up and spied her watching him at the window she'd nearly died, her face flushing wildly. He'd stared back at her for a few seconds, before whirling away and striding off inside the pool house.

Paige hadn't needed another sign.

Suddenly, she couldn't wait to finish school, or for him to say something. She had to speak up first. But when she'd gone in search of him after breakfast it had been to find her father and his assistant had left on a business trip. They would not be back for a week. It had been the longest week of Paige's life, only made bearable by the heart to hearts she'd had with Brad, her oldest and closest friend.

By the time Antonio had come back she'd been dying to talk to him, breathless and emboldened by the surety of his love.

Oddly enough, Paige could no longer recall exactly what she'd said to him. Or what he'd said back. The only words which lived on in her memory were his calling her a silly little girl. They remained very clear, as did the overwhelming wave of humiliation which had accompanied them.

Suffice to accept that it had been the most awful moment of her life.

Paige found it ironic that she didn't rate what had happened last night to be nearly as awful. Jed might have hurt her physically, and he'd frightened her enough into coming home, but he didn't have the power to hurt her where the hurt never healed. How could he, when she didn't love him?

Her right hand lifted to push her hair back behind her ear before gingerly touching the tender swelling just below her temple. Pity the blow hadn't knocked some sense into her, she thought bitterly.

Still being in love with Antonio was insane. She could see that. But recognising the stupidity of her feelings seemed to make no difference.

Brad had talked her out of her 'infatuation' for a while, had made her temporarily believe it was nothing but a schoolgirl crush, a romantic obsession which had nothing to do with reality.

'You don't even know the man,' he'd reasoned with her during the dark days after Antonio's visit to the beach-house. 'Your love's a figment of your romantic teenage imagination, conjured up because you need someone to love, and to love you back. But it's not real, Paige. It's a destructive self-indulgence to keep harbouring such a one-sided obsession. Let it go, love. Let *him* go.'

So she had, for a while, and eventually she'd settled for a different sort of love with Brad than the one she'd dreamt of in Antonio's arms.

Still, looking back, she did not regret it. Brad had been kind to her. Kind and understanding and undemanding. He'd taught her a lot about the sort of person she was, made her see that she was very intelligent, despite not having done too well at school. He'd even encouraged her to go to the local tech and finish her schooling, which she had. She might still have been with him if one stormy afternoon and an unforgiving sea hadn't ended their carefree and easygoing co-existence.

She'd stayed on at the beach-house for a few weeks. Brad had always paid the rent ahead in three-month lots. But in the end loneliness—and curiosity, perhaps—had sent her back home to Sydney, to Fortune Hall, her father, and Antonio.

A *big* mistake.

For nothing had changed.

Nothing.

She hadn't been able to get out of the place fast enough, answering an ad in the paper to share a flat with two other girls and taking the first job she could get, waitressing in a coffee house on Circular Quay.

Another big mistake. Not the job. She'd rather liked waitressing, enjoying the contact with tourists and people always on the go. Paige had soon found, however, that sharing accommodation with other girls was hazardous in the extreme, unless you looked like the back of a bus. Unfortunately, Paige's long blond hair, pretty face and striking figure had caused all sorts of troubles with the other girls' boyfriends, who hadn't been able to keep their eyes and hands off. After one extremely unpleasant encounter—and a disbelieving flatmate—Paige had found herself out on the street with nowhere to go except home once more.

This time Antonio had no longer been in residence, thanks to a promotion and a new apartment of his own somewhere.

Perversely, Paige had been disappointed. Had she become addicted to the emotional turmoil the sight of her unrequited love caused?

Possibly, because after leaving home again, to live

with two male flatmates who had been closet gays and had caused her no trouble at all, she'd still deliberately returned at Christmas—and every Christmas after that—for no other reason than that was the season her father entertained a lot, with dinner parties and other larger parties, to which Antonio was always invited.

She had seen him a few times, but he'd invariably ignored her, or just said a few polite words before turning his attention elsewhere, usually to some woman. Paige knew he had lots of women—she'd made a point of questioning a few of the staff at home about his dating activities. Not Evelyn, of course. But the cook, the maids, and Jim, the chauffeur.

Paige consoled herself with the thought that there never seemed to be anyone special, anyone who lasted. On top of that, she'd never experienced the agony of actually seeing him in action with a woman...till last year's big Christmas Eve party.

Paige had turned twenty-two the previous October, and believed she'd never looked better. Her skin had been lightly tanned, and her long honey-blond hair fell halfway down her back in one smooth shiny curtain. She'd come downstairs, dressed in a very sexy strapless red dress, hoping against hope that this time Antonio might see that she was at last a woman, not a silly little girl.

Antonio had just arrived with a date, a striking and sophisticated creature of thirty-something who had still made Paige feel like a little girl by comparison. His gaze had skated over her—and her revealing dress—with nothing but barely held irritation.

Never had the futility of her feelings been hammered home so strongly as that evening, when she'd watched him turn from her to dance attendance on his date, never once giving Paige a second glance. Each touch of his hand on the woman's arm had been like a dagger in Paige's heart. Each drink he'd given her. Each dance.

But the *coup de grâce* had come when Paige came across them kissing on the terrace—if 'kissing' was the appropriate word to describe what they'd been doing. For it hadn't just been their mouths which were locked, but their whole bodies. Moulded and melded together in the most erotic fashion, one of Antonio's legs jammed hard between the woman's, one of hers lifting to run sinuously up and down his thigh.

Paige was sure she'd cried out in pain, but nothing short of an atomic bomb exploding would have disturbed their passionate clinch. No one but the most naive could not imagine how their evening would end, or that Antonio wouldn't be the most unforgettable of lovers.

But then, Paige had already known he would be.

It was that same intense, all-consuming passion she'd thought she'd found in Jed. Only this time it had been directed at *her*, not some other woman. She'd been so flattered by Jed's pursuit of her. Flattered, yet disastrously deluded.

Paige winced as she touched the bruise once more.

She was about to go into the bathroom and inspect the damage more closely when there was a knock on her bedroom door.

'Who is it?' she asked agitatedly. Not her father again. Oh, please not him. He'd harangued her for ages last night, wanting to know what had happened, who had done this to her, what was his name, and his address? Had she been living with him? Was he her boyfriend, her lover? What had she done to make him hit her? She must have done something!

Dismay had kept her silent, and defiant, as usual.

She'd speared her father with a coldly contemptuous gaze before finally escaping to her room, only to fall onto the bed and cry herself to sleep. But now she was conscious again, and the transitory peace of oblivion was no longer hers.

'It's Evelyn. I've brought you up a tray.'

The door swung open before Paige could say another word, and in swept Evelyn. She was dressed in the same sort of bleak black dress she practically always wore, as though it were required uniform for a housekeeper. Paige noticed that she'd put on more weight this past year. Her cheeks had become jowly, and her already small eyes looked smaller within her pudgy face.

'Your father said you were not to be allowed to skip meals while you're here this time,' Evelyn pronounced haughtily as she placed the tray on the bedside table. 'He expects to hear that you've eaten every bite. And he expects to see you downstairs for dinner tonight as well. Right on eight. In a dress,' she added, throwing a derisive glance over Paige's jeans.

'I didn't bring any dresses with me,' Paige said, already regretting her decision to come home, despite not having any other real alternative this time. She needed the safety and security Fortune Hall provided, for she suspected Jed was not going to take her leaving him lightly.

'Don't be ridiculous, Paige,' came the sneering retort. 'You left a whole wardrobe full of clothes behind when you first left home. I moved them all into the guest room next door when I thought you weren't coming back and this room needed a thorough spring clean. There's plenty of dresses among them.'

'For pity's sake, Evelyn,' Paige pointed out wearily,

'you can't expect me to wear the same clothes I wore at seventeen.'

'Why not? I seem to recall you spent all that year buying and wearing clothes that were way too old for you. On top of that,' Evelyn added drily, 'if there's one thing I've learned since working for the rich and famous, it's that designer clothes don't date all that much. I'm sure you'll find something among them that'll do. It's not as though you've put on any weight. You're as skinny as ever.'

Evelyn had always made comments about her weight and Paige hated it. She was a tall girl, and naturally slim. But one could hardly call her 'skinny'.

'Whatever you say, Evelyn.' She was too tired of spirit to argue. And what did it really matter?

Evelyn went to leave, then stopped, peering closely at Paige's face. 'That's a nasty bruise you've got there, dear,' she said, with a malicious glint in those beady eyes of hers. 'Walk into a door?'

'Something like that.'

'You should watch where you're going, or one day you might really get hurt.' And, with an expression which implied such a prospect would please her no end, Evelyn exited the room, deliberately leaving the door open behind her.

Sighing, Paige rose and closed the door before returning to see what Evelyn had brought her to eat. Two huge club sandwiches, stuffed with mayonnaise. A piece of cream-filled cake big enough to feed an army, and a huge chocolate milkshake.

Paige knew she wouldn't be able to consume that amount, let alone such rich food. But she didn't dare leave any behind. Evelyn would report back to her father, who would lecture her on everything from anorexia to ingratitude. Defiance always had its price around Fortune Hall.

If only Blackie were still alive, she thought wistfully as she flushed half of the food down the toilet. That dog had been the perfect garbage disposal.

Paige's heart turned over as she thought of her long-deceased pet. As dogs went, Blackie had been exceedingly ugly: a flea-bitten mongrel Paige had rescued from the pound after they'd put his photograph in the Sunday papers. Her father had been furious when she'd bought him and brought him home. Blackie had almost been as old as she was. Seven to her nine. Her father had declared him a health hazard because he was recovering from mange. He'd told her that if she returned him he would get her a proper pup, a poodle with a pedigree and papers.

But she'd dug her heels in—the forerunner of future rebellions—and said stubbornly that she wasn't taking Blackie back to die and that she'd look after him herself, using her weekly allowance. He'd cost her a small fortune in vet bills, but she'd managed. Dog and girl had been inseparable till that dreadful day when she'd had to leave for boarding school. The housekeeper had promised to look after him, but when Paige had come back on her first home weekend, a month later, Evelyn had been installed as the new housekeeper and Blackie was declared dead, supposedly run over by a car. She'd never quite believed this story, but could never prove otherwise.

Paige had vowed to get herself another dog one day. But she never had. It was hard to risk one's heart a second time after being so badly hurt, she'd found. Very hard.

With half the food flushed away, and the rest reluctantly stuffed down into her fragile-feeling stomach, Paige went along to the next room to review the dresses that had appealed to her seventeen-year-old taste.

She shook her head over most of them. If ever she needed evidence of her schoolgirl obsession with Antonio, it was in the collection of clothes before her. Never had she seen such an array of painfully provocative purchases: all designed to flaunt her body, and all, as Evelyn had pointed out, way too old for a seventeen-year-old.

No wonder Antonio had stared at her across the dinner table when she'd come down dressed in those. Any living, breathing man would have given her a second glance. Paige was not ignorant of her physical attractions. She'd had them thrown in her face often enough in the past few years.

Her hand ran along the hangers, searching for something—*anything*—which was suitable for a simple dinner with her father. She bypassed everything which was too short, too clingy, or too low-cut.

Her eye finally landed on a cornflower-blue trouser suit which she'd never actually worn at all, come to think of it. She'd bought it at one of those end-of-season sales because the saleslady had raved about her in it. But when she'd got it home Paige had childishly thought it far too simple and plain.

Now, she liked its elegant simplicity very much. And blue always looked good on her, with her fair hair and blue eyes. But it wasn't a dress, was it? Too bad, she decided mutinously, and tugged the hanger out.

Fortunately, the left-behind shoes didn't present any choice problem at all. Paige had been five-nine by the time she was fourteen, so she'd never bought too high a heel, not even during her Antonio-mad year.

Selecting a pair of open-toed cream shoes with a low-ish heel, she returned to her room, where she stripped down to her undies and tried on the trouser suit. The reflection in the full-length cheval mirror in the corner brought an instant frown. Dear heaven, but she looked terribly busty! Bras did that to her in some clothes. Taking off the cardigan-style top, she removed her bra, then slid the silky cardigan back on, doing up the three small pearl buttons and having another look.

Much, much better. Her breasts looked smaller for having settled lower and wider apart on her chest, and there wasn't an in-your-face cleavage filling the deep V-neckline. There were no ugly bra lines, either, to mar the way the silky top smoothly outlined her bust before falling loosely to her hips. The trousers had a similar cut, fitting snugly around her hips before falling straight down to her ankles in softer folds. It was a very wearable and comfortable outfit which would fit a wide variety of occasions. She really must remember to take it with her when she next left.

Whenever that would be...

Paige hadn't just lost the roof over her head last night. She'd lost her clothes as well. Which was a pity. She'd spent quite a bit putting together a decent work wardrobe to go with her new career direction.

If only she'd dared go back into Jed's bedroom and get her set of keys before sneaking out of the place. If she had, she'd be able to slip into the building—and the apartment—while Jed was at work.

Paige sighed. She could hardly see herself showing up while Jed was home, and politely asking permission to come up and get the rest of her clothes. Better she cut her losses and just disappeared.

Maybe it was time to head interstate. Maybe up north

to Queensland, where there were plenty of holiday resorts, and plenty of jobs going for an attractive girl with a wide range of working experience.

A move to Queensland, however, would require money for her fare and some new clothes. She had some savings, but would need every cent to set herself up in a flat. Bond money and such. Her father would give her money if she asked, Paige knew. He might even resume putting that obscene monthly allowance into her bank account, if she begged.

Frankly, she was tempted. All she had to do was eat humble pie and tell her father he was the greatest.

But then she would have nothing left, would she? No self-respect. No independence. No pride.

She had to find some other way out of the hell-hole she'd dug for herself this time. Maybe she could stay here for a while, and get a job which had a uniform and gradually put together a wardrobe. She supposed she could bear Evelyn and her father for a few weeks. And at least she had one decent interview outfit!

Paige stripped off again and headed for the bathroom. Time to have a long, relaxing bath. Time to pretend she hadn't totally stuffed up her life once more. Time to transport herself to a world where the man she was with would never dream of raising his hand to her, where the rings on her left hand spoke of love and commitment, and the babies they made together would never know the hurt and unhappiness which had marred her own childhood.

When at her lowest, Paige always kept herself sane by wallowing in just such a fantasy world. So she lay there for ages beneath the lavender-scented bubble bath she'd found in the vanity and conjured up old faces, old dreams, and old desires. Time flew by, and if, eventually, tears rolled down Paige's cheeks, her soul had still been strangely soothed by her imaginings.

At five to eight that evening, Paige carried her softened and perfumed body slowly down the huge sweeping staircase, crossed the cavernous foyer, with its domed, chandeliered ceiling, and entered the huge living area which led into the smaller and more elegant room where her father always had pre-dinner drinks. He did this for half an hour before every meal, regardless of whether he had visitors or not. Paige never joined him, partly because she didn't like to drink on an empty stomach, but mainly because she didn't like to give her father the opportunity to hurt her. When he drank, he developed a sarcastic tongue.

Given that it was a Monday, Paige assumed he would be alone. So when she opened the door which led into the drawing room she was startled to see that wasn't the case at all.

No...*startled* did not adequately describe her reaction to the sight of an elegantly attired Antonio, sitting in one of the armchairs which flanked the fireplace, a crystal flute of champagne in his hands. *Stunned* better described her instant state of mind. Stunned and sickened.

Antonio was the last man in the world she wanted to see again, especially tonight, with the mark of another man's contempt for her glowering angrily on her cheekbone.

CHAPTER THREE

FOR a few fraught, fragile moments, Paige just stared at Antonio. Hard not to when the sight of him had always made her heart hammer madly against her ribs.

This time was no different, except that her head began whirling angrily at the same time. Why hadn't Evelyn warned her Antonio would be here for dinner? She must have known he was coming.

The answer was obvious, and cruel.

Because she didn't want you to be prepared. She wanted you to stumble in here and make a fool of yourself, as you always do in Antonio's presence.

Paige knew there wasn't anything that happened around Fortune Hall which Evelyn wasn't privy to. What the housekeeper didn't come to know by virtue of her position she found out through slyness and stealth. Over the years, Paige had caught the woman eavesdropping more than once, especially on the telephone. Her omission to mention Antonio's presence at dinner could only have had a malicious intent, which meant the hateful woman was aware of Paige's feelings for Antonio.

Pride came to the rescue, as did some hard-won experience. Maybe she was getting used to handling the emotional devastation seeing Antonio always caused her. Or was it that at last she was beginning to grow up?

'Why, hello, Antonio,' she said casually as she strolled into the room and over towards the drinks cabinet in the corner. 'You startled me there for a moment. No one said anything about you being here tonight.

You're looking well,' she added, somewhat tongue-in-cheek. *Well* was not a word one would use to describe Antonio. It was far too insipid for his brand of raw physical impact.

Tonight, he was looking exceptionally sexy all in black, his fine woollen suit given a casual look by being teamed with a black crew-necked top rather than his usual shirt and tie. The outfit seemed to intensify his dark colouring and brooding sex appeal, a fact which certainly didn't escape Paige's poor, pathetic heart.

'I was thinking the same of you, actually,' he returned silkily. 'Considering…'

She laughed, sliding a mocking glance over her shoulder at him. 'You mean for someone who's boyfriend has just beaten her up?' Paige had found over the last few years that being mealy-mouthed and defensive around Fortune Hall only brought more looks and lectures on the way she was living her life. Better to face any sticky situation head-on, with a suitably defiant façade.

'Paige, for pity's sake!' her father protested.

'*Pity*, Father?' she scoffed as she swept the bottle of champagne from the ice bucket and poured herself a glass. Suddenly, drinking on an empty stomach was not only desirable but imperative!

'Now that's a word I've not heard often in this house,' she muttered, and turned back round, the crystal flute cupped firmly in her hands, her knuckles white in the effort to stop them from shaking. 'So what have you been drinking to with this very expensive champagne? I can't imagine its your health. You'll both still be taking the television world by storm when I'm six foot under.'

Her gaze swept over the two men, who stared back at her with perfect poker faces, telling her nothing, and everything. 'Oh, I see,' she said drily. 'It's a secret, is it? Something to do with business. Something silly little girls like me couldn't possibly understand, or shouldn't know.'

Paige was surprised to see her spiked sarcasm brought a wry smile to Antonio's beautifully shaped mouth. 'Not at all,' he said. 'I'm sure your father wouldn't mind your knowing.'

Did Antonio see the warning glance her father shot him? If he did, he ignored it.

'We're celebrating a forthcoming and hopefully desirable merger,' he went on smoothly, his black eyes glittering with some secret amusement. Or was it suppressed anger? One could never quite tell with Antonio. 'Unfortunately, negotiations are at too early and too delicate a stage to supply you with more details right now.'

'How delightfully vague!' she exclaimed, rolling her eyes at him. She should have known Antonio wouldn't cross her father. He knew what side his bread was buttered on.

Not that Antonio was easily cast in the role of flunkey. He was far too strong-willed and opinionated to be a mindless yes-man. She'd heard him disagree with her father more than once when it came to business.

But she was still piqued that he felt he could play with words around her. It was so patronising. And so like the treatment she'd always received around Fortune Hall. If she'd been born a boy she would have been drawn into their world of negotiations and deals, not excluded, then cynically condescended to!

Her eyes flashed as she lifted her glass in a mock toast. 'To the forthcoming and hopefully...what kind of merger did you say it was, Antonio?'

'Desirable,' he said quietly, and that inscrutable black gaze of his ran slowly over her from head to toe.

Paige's heart tripped, then stopped altogether when those eyes began to travel back up her body even more slowly, lingering on the swells and dips of her female form, leaving them burning in his wake. He inspected her mouth for what felt like an interminable length of time, forcing her lips to fall apart and drag in some much needed air for her starving lungs.

Now his eyes lifted to hers, holding them in a hard and merciless gaze which was as blatantly sexual as it was chillingly cold.

She quivered. All over. Inside and out.

It was the most erotic thing which had ever happened to her.

Her heart began to race, an uncomfortable heat suffusing her skin.

Paige did the only thing she could think of to survive the moment. She quaffed back the chilled champagne she was holding. The whole lot.

Unfortunately, her ragged breathing sent some down the wrong way and she began to choke.

Antonio was beside her in a flash, slapping her firmly between the shoulders. The champagne came flying back up and sprayed out from her mouth, most of it falling to the carpet but some dribbling down her front.

'Try to breathe slowly and evenly,' Antonio advised, once she'd stopped choking to death.

She tried, but it was almost impossible with him standing so close to her, then perfectly impossible when Antonio drew a snow-white handkerchief from his trouser pocket and started wiping down her top where the champagne had stained it, stroking the handkerchief down over the swell of her right breast, working his way closer and closer to her hardening nipple. As he drew dangerously close she felt her flesh tighten even further in anticipation of his touch, craving the contact, practically begging for it.

Paige sucked in sharply when the handkerchief finally slid over the tautened peak, her head spinning wildly. He did it again. Then again.

Confusion flung her eyes wide to search his. Was he being deliberately cruel? Did he have any idea what he was doing to her? She dared not believe this was real, but when their eyes met Paige was stunned to see he was as enthralled as she was by what he was doing.

The handkerchief came to rest over the traitorous peak, hiding it from sight. 'Do you want to go upstairs and change?' he asked her in a low, thickened voice.

'I...I don't have anything to change into,' came her shaky reply, and Antonio frowned.

'There's no *time* to change,' Conrad snapped irritably, from where he'd risen and was moving towards the now open dining room door. 'Dinner's ready to be served.'

'Why don't you have anything to change into?' Antonio asked in a disconcertingly gentle tone as he led her still shaken self to her place at the table. 'Or don't you want to tell me?'

Suddenly, she *did* want to tell him. Suddenly, he wasn't the disapproving, remote, unattainable man he'd become over the years. He was more like that other Antonio Scarlatti, the one who'd kindly met her train that day, and started her obsession with him.

Was one of her futile dreams in danger of coming true? Had Antonio finally seen her tonight as a grown-up woman, and not a silly little girl?

'Later,' she whispered to him when he pulled her seat out for her.

His breath was warm against her ear as he scooped

her chair under her. 'I'll look forward to it,' he murmured, and she quivered helplessly.

Dinner was agony. And ecstasy. One minute she would be smiling and sparkling at him, then doubts would besiege her and she'd fall worriedly silent. Why now? she agonised. Why tonight? Did her father have anything to do with this? Had he ordered Antonio to be nice to her?

No, no, that couldn't be it, she decided at long last. If Antonio's ambitions lay in that direction, he would not have waited this long to pursue her. No, he was genuinely attracted to her tonight. She could feel it. There was a predatory glitter in his eyes, eyes which didn't stop looking at her. Paige knew what it was like to be the object of a man's sexual interest, and she could feel Antonio's desire hitting her in waves.

He wanted to make love to her.

The thought was breathtaking. And compellingly exciting.

It was only a sexual thing, of course. Paige was not naive enough to think anything else. Antonio was a man of the world, a confirmed bachelor type whose commitment was to the company. His bed-partners were transitory, and replaceable, like her father's. According to the staff at Fortune Hall, Antonio hadn't brought the same woman to dinner, or a party there, in all the years of his employ. If Paige let him seduce her, he would promise her nothing but passing pleasures, followed by the ultimate in pains.

But, oh…those passing pleasures…

Paige could barely begin to imagine them.

The ultimate in pains, however, she *could* imagine.

She groaned a silent groan. She'd have to be crazy to set herself up for that!

'Paige!' her father snapped. 'Evelyn's asking you if you want some dessert. What's the matter with you tonight, girl? One minute chattering away sixty to the dozen, the next off in some dream world!'

Her blue eyes cleared to see the hated housekeeper smirking at her from her position at her father's shoulder.

'No dessert, thank you,' Paige said stiffly, while she struggled to suppress the overwhelmingly negative feelings the woman always evoked in her.

'You're not becoming anorexic again, are you?' her father demanded, exasperation in his voice.

'I was *never* anorexic!' she defended hotly. 'I have no idea where you ever got such an idea,' she finished, whilst looking daggers at Evelyn.

The housekeeper's beady eyes didn't move an inch.

'Then prove it by having some apple crumble!' her father insisted. 'Bring Paige a large helping, Evelyn. With plenty of cream.'

A helpless fury flooded Paige as the housekeeper swanned off with a triumphant expression on her face. If Antonio hadn't been at the table she would have left the room. Instead, she was stuck there, feeling belittled and foolish. She could not bear to look over at Antonio, afraid to see his earlier attraction for her had faded because she was being treated like a difficult and wayward child.

'The reason Paige probably turned dessert down, Conrad,' Antonio said, and Paige's eyes snapped up to stare across the table at him, 'is because she promised to have supper with me later. I should have said no to dessert as well.'

Paige was as amazed as her father by this announceme**a**t. She'd only agreed to *talk* to Antonio later. Nothing more. But she wasn't about to say anything. Not now.

'You and Paige are having supper together?' her father challenged. *'Tonight?'*

Antonio didn't look at all concerned by his employer's tone of disapproval. 'I trust you have no objection to that?' he returned, an icy counter-challenge in his voice.

Paige was mesmerised by the exchange.

'No, no, I suppose not. It's just that…well…I'm surprised, that's all.'

No more than herself, Paige thought dazedly.

'You only flew into town this morning,' her father went on a little testily. 'I would have thought you'd be too tired to go out.'

'I slept on the plane,' Antonio explained coolly. 'I'm only home for two weeks, as you know. Terrible to waste my holiday sleeping it away, don't you think? There are much better ways to spend one's leisure time. What say you, Paige? Should we make our escape now, before Evelyn returns and force-feeds us both?'

Paige didn't need any encouragement. She was on her feet in a flash. Too late, however. Evelyn was already coming into the room, carrying a tray of desserts towards the table.

Paige hesitated. Not so Antonio, who strode around the table towards her.

'Our apologies, Evelyn,' he said smoothly as he took Paige's elbow and steered her towards the doorway. 'Paige and I are going out and haven't time for dessert right now.'

Paige expected the woman to look put out. Instead, she smiled oh, so sweetly at them both as they passed.

'That's quite all right, Antonio. Dessert will keep. It's nice to see you and Paige are friends at long last.'

Paige's mouth dropped open at Evelyn's hypocrisy. There was no level to which that woman would not stoop!

'Don't wait up, Conrad,' Antonio called back, with a nonchalant glance over his shoulder. 'And don't worry. Your daughter will be perfectly safe in my hands.'

CHAPTER FOUR

ANTONIO almost laughed at the expression on Conrad's face. It seemed it was one thing to callously blackmail an employee into bedding and wedding your wayward daughter, quite another to witness the process first hand.

Antonio suspected his employer might be having second thoughts.

But it was too late now. The wheels had been set in motion, and Antonio meant to see the journey through to the bitter end.

'My car's outside,' he told Paige as he urged her across the living room floor towards the foyer.

She nodded, but said nothing, which was fine by him. He wanted to get her out of the house as quickly as possible. No way did he want Conrad trying to stop things now, just because he'd had a momentary flutter of conscience, or because the reality of an illegitimate Italian peasant seducing his daughter stuck in his throat.

Actually, Antonio found this evening's events perverse in the extreme. He'd fumed all day over being backed into such a corner, arriving for drinks and dinner tonight in a smouldering state of black fury. Only the thought of Brock Masters being handed the job which *he'd* worked so darned hard for had stopped Antonio from throwing the cold-blooded bargain back in Conrad's face.

But the moment he'd set eyes on Paige this evening, looking surprisingly elegant and incredibly sexy, his male hormones had kicked in, and Antonio had decided a man's fate could be worse than having such a delectable creature as his wife for a while.

But only for a while.

Antonio had no intention of staying married to the girl. Which was one little loophole his employer hadn't thought of. Nowhere did the promissory letter in Antonio's pocket say he would lose his job as CEO if he divorced Paige. He would make sure that the contract he signed on his wedding day was irretrievable and unbreakable, no matter what!

Of course, that still left the problem of getting Paige to marry him in the first place. Antonio had no doubt he could get the girl into bed with him in no time. Dear Lord, she *was* a push-over where the opposite sex was concerned. He'd only had to make eye contact with her a few times tonight, and she'd been his for the taking.

Admittedly, she exuded a pretty powerful chemistry of her own. Once those big blue eyes had clamped on to his, he'd found it difficult to keep his mind—and his body—on track. When he'd been wiping down that top of hers he'd almost forgotten who was seducing whom.

But getting the man-mad Paige into bed was a far cry from getting her to agree to marry him. She hadn't married any of her other lovers, had she? Why should he be any different? It was naive of Conrad to think a schoolgirl crush was the same as being seriously in love. Antonio doubted Paige had ever been seriously in love in her life.

Get her pregnant had been Conrad's ruthless suggestion. Antonio wondered if his boss was still so keen on *that* idea.

Antonio didn't fancy it at all, though he could see it might become his final option. He would certainly try the whirlwind romance bit first. And plenty of sex. Oh, yes, definitely plenty of sex. Hell, he hadn't been this turned on in years!

But the bottom line was Paige had a mind of her own, a stubborn, rebellious, changeable mind, and she obviously had a low boredom threshold when it came to the men in her life. She'd promised *him* undying love and devotion once, a promise which had lasted all of a week or two. Loyal wife material she was not.

But marry her he would, by hook or by crook!

His hand tightened on her arm and she threw him a look which almost stopped him in his tracks.

For never had Antonio seen such vulnerability in a woman's eyes. Or such sweet gratitude.

His gaze dropped to the ugly bruise on her cheek, and that sometimes awkward conscience of his raised its infernal interfering head. How could he ruthlessly seduce her later tonight when she was looking at him as though he were a hero, rescuing her from the villains of this world? Couldn't she see that *he* was the villain this time?

But, damn it all, what was the alternative? Leave her to Brock 'Marquis de Sade' Masters? Compared to Masters, he *was* a hero.

Besides, it wasn't as though he was going to hurt the girl. He was going to be very nice to her, make beautiful love to her, tell her he loved her.

Lie to her, you mean, came the brutal voice of honesty.

'Antonio?' Conrad called from the dining room, his voice gruff. 'Antonio! Are you still there by any chance?'

Antonio hesitated, but Paige left him to run over to the security panel behind the front door. 'Hurry,' she urged as she punched in the gate code.

His black Jaguar was waiting, like Lochinvar's trusty

steed. They dashed down the steps and dived into their respective seats as one, slamming the car doors behind them and tugging on their seat belts.

'Don't stop for anything,' his breathtakingly beautiful and stunningly sexy passenger advised as he gunned the engine.

'Don't worry,' Antonio muttered, his body making his decision for him. 'I won't.'

The car screeched off, gravel spraying out behind them. The die was cast. There was no going back.

CHAPTER FIVE

PAIGE'S heart accelerated with the car as it sped around the circular drive and shot through the gates. The tyres squealed when they hit the road at an angle, but Antonio corrected the small skid and pointed the Jaguar towards the city centre.

'You can let go of the seat belt now,' he said, with dry amusement in his voice, and Paige saw she was indeed gripping it across her chest, as a child might grip the security bar on one of those wild fairground rides.

But in truth that was how she felt, as though she'd jumped onto a runaway rollercoaster which was in danger of hurtling out of control.

'What do you think Father wanted you for?' she asked breathlessly.

'Probably something to do with business. It can wait,' he pronounced, with a confidence Paige could not help but admire.

There again, there was so much to admire about Antonio. And she wasn't just talking about his looks, although he was still one of the handsomest men she'd ever met. Antonio was an enigma, in a way. A man of contradictions. Privately passionate, Paige had no doubt. But with a public and professional self-possession she could only envy. If only she had half as much control over her own emotions. And her life.

This last thought brought her back to earth with a jolt. What *was* she doing here with Antonio, letting her feelings for him run away with her common sense again,

49

agreeing to a date which could only have one motivation and one ending?

That was a part of Antonio which wasn't so admirable. His treatment of women. He never let a woman into his life, except briefly, and then only on a superficial sexual level.

Which was probably why her father hadn't liked their going off together at this hour of the night. No doubt he knew exactly how Antonio's supper dates usually ended, and, whilst Paige didn't believe her father gave a damn about Antonio's personal morals, he probably didn't like to see his own daughter being used in such a fashion. It wasn't a matter of parental caring—when had her father ever really cared about her?—but male ego. Her father was always going on about her making a fool of herself over men, simply because he was afraid her behaviour might somehow reflect on him. He was probably worrying it might be awkward to face Antonio at the office in future, knowing the other man had *known* his daughter.

Known...

Paige's throat thickened at the thought.

The Bible had a way of saying something which sounded like a euphemism, but which was, in fact, incredibly explicit. If she went to bed with Antonio, he would know her as no man had ever known her before. For, although she wasn't a physical virgin, she was still very much an emotional virgin. She'd never given her all to a man, had she? Never given her heart and soul along with her body.

But she would with Antonio, wouldn't she?

How could she not?

And when she did, what would he see? What would he *know*?

'Father seemed a little worried about our going out together,' she choked out, echoing her own inner misgivings.

'He'll get used to the idea.'

Paige blinked, then turned her head slowly to stare at Antonio. 'What...what do you mean?'

'Exactly that. Recognising that one's daughter is finally a grown woman is hard for most fathers. Even yours, Paige.'

'He's always thought of me as a silly little girl,' she said bitterly. 'As did you, Antonio.'

'Never!' he denied.

Shock was mixed with confusion. 'How can you *say* that?'

He shrugged. 'Quite easily. Because it's true.'

She shook her head vehemently. 'That's not what you said to me that day by the pool. And it's not what's been in your eyes every time we've met since then.'

'Ah, but Paige, you should never try to read a man's eyes. It's his body language you must learn to take note of. Believe me when I say I've never thought of you as anything but the most irritatingly attractive female.'

'Irritating?'

'Well, of course! How would you expect a lowly employee to view the boss's beautiful daughter, especially when she was only seventeen? No matter how I felt about you that day by the pool, I couldn't in all conscience do anything about it, could I?'

Paige's breath caught. 'Are you saying you *did* feel something?'

He flashed her the sexiest of smiles. 'Let's just say I was eternally grateful there was a towel between us.'

Paige's heart fell. Sex. That was what he was talking about. That was all he'd felt for her. That was all *most* men felt for her. She should have known better than to hope for anything more, even for a second.

'I'm sure you didn't suffer for too long,' she bit out. 'A man like you would never be wanting for that kind of company.'

'Nor a girl like you,' he retaliated, the counter-attack not sitting well with her.

As usual, when hurt, Paige laughed, then went on the offensive. 'How right you are! But be fair, Antonio, I haven't been seventeen for quite some time.'

His black eyes flicked her way, glittering and hard as they raked over her. 'Your father mentioned you turn twenty-three next week. What day, exactly?'

'Wednesday.'

'We'll have to do something special for you.'

Paige stiffened. If by *we* he meant he was going to talk her father into having Evelyn organise some ghastly party, then he could think again!

'Unless you've already got plans, of course?'

'No,' she said coldly. 'No plans.' But there would be no party!

'The boyfriend isn't going to be forgiven?'

The insensitive question infuriated Paige. 'Are you serious? You think I'd go back to some man who did this to me?' And she pushed her hair back behind her ear to show him the full extent of the bruise.

To give him credit, his eyes *did* show something this time. Although their expression conveyed more anger than sympathy.

'I should hope not,' he grated out. 'But women have been known to return to violent situations. God knows why!'

'Perhaps they have nowhere else to go.'

'Don't give me that, Paige. That's just an excuse.

There's always somewhere else to go. Women are their own worst enemies sometimes.'

'What would *you* know about being a woman, or what it's like to be female and afraid? It's easy for you to make snap judgements from behind your six-foot frame and macho muscles.'

'If you say so,' he remarked drily. 'I really don't wish to discuss this subject other than to find out who did that to you. And don't even *consider* defending him, Paige.'

'I won't. But, frankly, it's none of your business, just as it was none of my father's business.'

'I beg to differ. Men like your bullying boyfriend make the rest of my sex look bad. They can't be allowed to get away with thinking they can beat up their girl-friends, no matter what she does or says to provoke him.'

'He didn't beat me up. He only hit me once.'

'Once is enough. If you'd stayed, the next time it would have been worse.'

'Why do you think I left?' she snapped.

'So what set him off?' Antonio persisted. 'What *did* you do?'

'It wasn't what I did,' she muttered. 'But what I *didn't* do.'

'Meaning?'

Her stomach churned as she looked over at the man who was behind it all. How blissfully unaware he was, sitting there, probably thinking he was helping her. Yet, really, he was to blame. For everything.

Perhaps he was right to say that women were their own worst enemies. They often loved stupidly, without sufficient reason and without hope.

Suddenly, the urge to fling the truth at him was acute. And she almost did. But at the last moment she let her love for him lie hidden within her words.

'Jed had just had sex with me,' she said baldly instead. 'But I hadn't enjoyed it. He took it badly, and personally. He accused me of not loving him, of wanting some other man instead. When I didn't deny it, he lost his temper and hit me.'

Antonio was deathly silent for several excruciating seconds while the car stopped at a set of red lights, the engine idling like some snarling animal, poised and ready to pounce.

The man behind the wheel seemed just as tense. Paige gained the impression her confession had angered him. Yet, when he spoke, his voice was icy cool.

'That was a dangerous thing to do, Paige. A man's ego can be very fragile.'

'Only *some* men's, Antonio.'

His dark eyes narrowed on her. 'Did you provoke him like that because he was disappointing in bed and you wanted to end your relationship?'

She shrugged. 'What can I say? I realised I couldn't bear to have him touch me again, so I let him believe what he wanted to believe.'

'So there *isn't* some secret love, waiting in the wings to become your next conquest?'

'None but you, Antonio,' came her dry but perversely true comment.

His laugh carried just the right amount of return cynicism, letting her know that he hadn't twigged to the truth at all. The lights turned green and the car leapt forward, leaving Paige to live with the consequences of what she'd just done.

No doubt Antonio now thought she was a promiscuous little piece, going from man to man, moving on as soon as her lover began to bore her in bed. Little did he know that Jed was the first man she'd slept with since

Brad, all those years ago. Or that last night had been their first time together.

Still, perhaps it was better that Antonio thought she was a woman of the world, whose heart was rarely involved in her various dalliances. That way, if tonight ended as she suspected it might, she could pretend to be unaffected afterwards, and whenever she ran into him in the future.

Her eyes suddenly cleared to find they were crossing the bridge and heading towards the north side of the harbour.

'Where are you taking me?' she asked abruptly.

'Where would you like me to take you?'

'I thought we were going to supper somewhere. I imagined some place in the city.'

'I've decided to head for my apartment instead,' he returned, without missing a beat. 'It's only a couple of minutes from the city, and has several advantages over a nightclub. Firstly, it has free parking. Secondly, a view *par excellence*, not to mention a complete range of in-house services. I thought it would be very pleasant to complete supper on our own private balcony overlooking the harbour.'

'I'm sure it would.' After which, it was just a short stroll inside and into the bedroom. No doubt Antonio thought *that* the best advantage of all!

Paige tried to find the strength to tell him, no, she preferred somewhere far more public. But the devil was in her ear, along with her own traitorous weakness for the man.

Turn him down tonight and you might never have another chance. He's home on holiday, and wants a woman for the night. Maybe even for the whole fortnight! Fate threw you into his path this evening, Paige, and finally he noticed *you* were a woman.

Cynicism added that there had to be dozens of women in Sydney he could date instead, who would do admirably—women who would drop everything to be with him. He wouldn't suffer if she turned him down. And he wouldn't be alone. Men like Antonio were never alone when they didn't want to be.

Could she bear the knowledge that he was somewhere in Sydney, making love to some other woman when it could have been her? Could she lie in bed at night and sleep, craving him?

The simple answer was no. She could not.

'Is it far to your apartment?'

Antonio could hear the sexual tension in her voice and felt his own flesh prickle alarmingly.

He almost felt sorrow for the fellow she'd walked out on last night. No doubt he was crazy about her, and thought his feelings had been returned. Antonio could see the scenario now: Paige coldly turning from her lover while her body was still hot from his lovemaking and cruelly telling him he wasn't up to par.

Women like her could drive a man crazy. They wound a man up, promising so much with their eyes and their body language, not to mention their sheer physical beauty. It was criminal for Mother Nature to give one woman so many attributes.

Conrad's daughter was sheer feminine perfection, with not a single flaw visible to the eye. Her face was classically lovely, with fine bone structure and symmetrical features. Her forehead was high and wide, as were her eyes: big blue eyes with long, curling lashes. Her nose was narrow and straight, its slightly uptilted end bringing attention to the full mouth beneath. Her even, white teeth might have been due to good dentistry, but, if so, the dentist had done an excellent job. Her smile was as dazzling as the rest of her.

Of course, it was the rest of her which had often unravelled Antonio, and which was unravelling him at this moment. He could not wait to wallow in the lush sensuality of her body. To spread her hair out over his pillow, to bury his mouth in her breasts, to feel her legs entwine themselves around him as he sank deeper and deeper inside her.

Not long now, he told himself as he turned off the expressway and headed towards his apartment. The twenty-storey building was situated at the end of a cul-de-sac at Milson's Point, with the back of the block facing the harbour.

Antonio was only two streets away when his car phone buzzed. Scowling impatience, he pulled the Jag over to the curb to answer, snatching the receiver up and snarling, 'Scarlatti,' down the line at the same time. Truly, there were times when he would like to consign mobile phones to the bottom of the harbour!

'Conrad, here,' his employer replied curtly, startling Antonio. 'Don't let Paige know it's me on the line. Just wanted to call and let you know I was only putting on an act earlier tonight. Knowing Paige, it seemed a good ploy not to seem too keen about you two being together. Do you see what I mean?'

'Yes,' Antonio muttered. 'I see.' Talk about devious!

'How are things going? Are you taking her back to your place?'

Antonio practically ground his teeth. If Conrad was expecting a blow by blow account of his daughter's seduction then he was going to be very disappointed.

'Yes. Thank you for that information,' he said. 'Must go,' he added, and slammed the phone down.

'Who was that?' Paige asked. 'Or shouldn't I ask?'

Be damned if he was going to lie to her!

'Your father.'

'What did he want?'

'Just passing on something he considered important. You know your father.'

'Oh, yes,' she sighed. 'Business comes first. Always.'

Her head turned away to stare through the passenger window as he drove off, but the moment he turned into his street she suddenly sat forward in the seat, her head whipping back round. When the Jaguar shot down the short street and straight onto the ramp which led down to the underground car park beneath the apartment block, Antonio felt her eyes boring into him.

'Is this some kind of sick joke, Antonio?'

A quick glance sidewards showed unexpected alarm in her eyes. Frowning, he moved his eyes frontwards to safely negotiate the tricky circular driveway which wound its way down to the car park. Once there, he swiftly angled the Jaguar into one of his two private spots and switched off the engine. He was about to ask Paige what on earth she was talking about when she swept on, her face flushed and undeniably furious.

'I can't believe you would do something like this. Oh, I dare say Father's behind it. That was what that call was all about, wasn't it? He had that creep of a detective of his find out Jed's name and address. It's no more than I'd expected of him, but not you, Antonio! I didn't think *you'd* be involved in something this underhand. For pity's sake, if Father was determined to confront Jed about what happened last night, then so be it! But to trick me into coming here with you by pretending to ask me out is beyond the pale! I'm not going up to Jed's with you, so don't think you can make me!' she threw at him, her voice shaking with emotion.

It didn't take long for the penny to drop, and when it did Antonio experienced a rush of emotion himself. 'Are you saying the man who hit you lives here as well?'

Her eyes grew wide upon him. 'Are *you* saying you *really* live in this building?'

'I own one of the two penthouse apartments.'

She paled, then laughed. 'You've got to be joking!'

'Do I look like I'm joking?'

'No...' She began shaking her head, as though she could hardly believe it.

Antonio was also having a hard job believing it. Now he knew the identity of Paige's lover, and where he lived.

Jed, she'd called him.

Jed was not a common name. The man who owned the other penthouse apartment was Jed Waltham, a successful Sydney stockbroker. Antonio had naturally met him a few times, since they shared the same lift, and the pool on the roof. In his early thirties, Waltham was darkly good-looking, and had an ego you couldn't climb over.

'How long have you been living with Jed Waltham?' he asked, trying to come to terms with his feelings at actually knowing Paige's errant lover. It was one thing to scornfully imagine her cohabiting with some ne'er-do-well in a fleabitten flat in some grotty suburb. Quite another to picture her in a luxury penthouse, in a luxury bed, beneath the likes of Jed Waltham.

'You...you *know* Jed?' she asked, disbelief still in her eyes.

'Not to any great degree. But naturally we've met in the lift a few times, and around the pool once or twice.'

Her frown carried genuine puzzlement. 'The pool?'

'You didn't ever use the pool on the roof?'

'I…no… I…I only moved in with Jed yesterday.'

Stupidly, Antonio felt relief at this news. But he hadn't liked the thought of her being there with Jed Waltham while he'd been right next door.

'Had you been lovers long before that?'

'We…we'd been going out for a while,' she hedged, which could have meant anything.

'Where did you meet?'

'At work.'

Now it was Antonio's turn to frown with genuine puzzlement. Paige gave him a dry look.

'I see Father *hasn't* been having that flunkey of his follow me around lately. I thought he'd stopped, but I wasn't sure.' Paige inhaled, then exhaled a weary sigh. 'Frankly, I'm surprised Father bothered for so long. He doesn't give a fig for me.'

Antonio supposed the man *did* care about Paige, in his own weird way, but it was hardly the kind of caring a daughter would appreciate. Once again, a certain sympathy for the girl undermined Antonio's determination to keep his mind focused on what he had to do. But, damn it all, she was beginning to stir things in him. And not just the obvious.

His own sigh carried a whole host of feelings, none of which he was comfortable with.

'You don't have to feel badly for me, Antonio,' she said ruefully, and his eyes jerked round to stare at her. 'I've long come to terms with my father's non-existent feelings for me.'

Once again, Antonio began to feel sorry for her, which

annoyed him. Seduction, not sympathy, was his aim
here. 'You didn't answer my question,' he snapped.

'Which one was that?'

'About how you met Waltham?'

'Oh, that one. Well, as I said, we met at work. I was
doing a few weeks as a temp at his firm. And before
you ask I did a night course at tech during the first six
months of this year. I finally decided I couldn't spend
the rest of my life as a waitress. I needed a job where I
could make more money than to just make ends meet.
So I learnt word processing, and other secretarial duties,
then signed up at one of those agencies which find you
work. They suggested that I start out as a temp. Because
of my looks, they said I was a cert for a reception job.
When the receptionist at Waltham & Coates went on
maternity leave for three months, I applied for and got
the job.'

Antonio was surprised, and quietly impressed. It
seemed she *had* started growing up after all. 'When did
you start there?'

'The tenth of July. I finished up last Friday.'

'And moved in with the boss two days later,' he
mused aloud. In *that* she hadn't changed. There always
had to be some man in her life, didn't there?

'Which moves us into the territory of questions I'm
not going to answer,' she said, with a defiant toss of her
head. 'I repeat, my relationship with Jed is none of your
business, Antonio. Let's just say I thought he loved me.
But a man doesn't do this to the woman he loves, does
he?' And she held her hair back again, for him to see
the evidence of Waltham's violence.

Antonio's stomach tightened as he stared at the bruise,
which had become darker and uglier since he'd last
looked. Any empathy he might have momentarily felt

for Paige's ex-lover disappeared as he glanced from her physically damaged face into her emotionally damaged eyes.

'You're quite right,' he ground out. 'Nothing justifies that. Come on, Paige. Get out of the car. We're going upstairs.'

CHAPTER SIX

PAIGE froze, her back pressed against the leather, her hands gripping the seat belt once more, lest Antonio forcibly undo it and drag her out. 'No! I'm not going up there. You can't make me!'

'I'm not taking you up to Waltham's apartment. I'm taking you up to mine. Then *I'm* going over to Waltham's.'

'But...but what for?' she asked shakily.

'To get back your clothes, for one thing. And to have a quiet little word,' he added, in the kind of low, coolly civilised voice she imagined a clever hitman might use to lure his prey to their deaths.

A shiver ran down her spine as she realised Antonio didn't want a *quiet word* with Jed. He wanted to beat him to a pulp. The vengeful part of Paige wanted him to do just that. But her softer, more sympathetic side knew she'd seriously provoked Jed by not responding or co-operating with him, and then in not denying his accusations.

Not that those things justified hitting her.

'I can't let you do that, Antonio,' she said, almost regretfully.

'Do what?' he asked.

'You *know* what. You're going to pulverise Jed. I can see it in your eyes.'

'You can read me that well? My poker face must be slipping. But so what if I want to teach Waltham a lesson

63

he won't forget? Are you saying you don't want me to, that you still care about the creep?'

'No. But I do care about *you*.' Her eyes remained steady on his, despite her heart fluttering wildly inside. 'I don't want you having to answer to some assault charge because of me. I would really appreciate your getting my clothes. But for the rest...I would much prefer you left well enough alone, and came back to me safe and sound.'

Antonio didn't know if he felt triumphant or troubled. Nothing was going as planned. The Paige who'd always irritated him to death was now engaging far more than his carnal desires. He wanted to know more about her, wanted to put the pieces of her puzzle together.

What was real and what had he presumed? Was she shallow and silly, or sensitive and misunderstood? Was she genuinely promiscuous, or a love-starved woman, desperate to find some real affection from any man?

Antonio noted that most of her lovers had been some years older then herself. Perhaps she was looking for a father figure. Perhaps her never-ending bed-hopping was the result of a quest to find the sort of love she'd never had from Conrad.

Antonio appreciated that everyone who'd ever been emotionally neglected as a child craved love as one would crave a drug. He himself had once been needy in that regard. He'd thought he'd found the answer to his need in Lauren, lavishing all the love he'd had to give on her. But he'd been as deluded by Lauren as Paige had obviously been by Waltham.

He wished he knew *exactly* what had happened last night. He could not imagine a man like Waltham being an inadequate lover. If he *was* unsatisfactory in bed, then why had Paige moved in with him in the first place?

Unfortunately, Paige was not going to give him any details. She'd been adamant about that.

Whatever, Waltham was about to wish he hadn't struck Conrad Fortune's daughter.

Antonio had never told his neighbour what he did for a living, other than to make some casual remark about being in business. He always kept a low profile, media-wise, letting Conrad have all the limelight. Antonio wasn't into that kind of thing. He valued his privacy too much. Consequently, he could give his position at Fortune Productions any slant he wanted.

'Did Waltham know you were Conrad Fortune's daughter?' he asked abruptly.

'Heavens, no. I never tell anyone that! I'm not stupid, you know.'

'Stupid?'

'Aside from the security angle, I like to be liked for myself, thank you very much, not because I'm a rich man's daughter.'

Antonio found it ironic that her being a rich man's daughter had always been an obstacle in *his* liking her. Before tonight, that was. Tonight he was finding he liked Paige a lot. Far too much, actually. He would have preferred keeping his feelings for her firmly on a lust basis. Lust he was comfortable with. Lust he could handle.

'Are you coming up?' he said a touch sharply. 'Or are you going to just sit there and wait till I come back down with your clothes?'

'How do you know Jed's home?'

'That's his car over there, isn't it?' he said, and pointed to the red Ferrari in the next row.

Paige nodded.

'Then he's home. Men who drive Ferraris don't use taxis.'

Antonio waited while she gnawed at her bottom lip for a full ten seconds. 'You won't let him anywhere near me, will you?'

She really was frightened. 'You have my word,' he assured her, and hardened his resolve to give Jed Waltham a taste of his own medicine. And right where it hurt most!

Paige scooped in a deep breath before letting it out with a shudder. 'Okay, then.'

He deposited her safely in his apartment, with instructions not to answer the door to anyone. He told her to make herself comfortable. There was whatever she might wish to drink behind the bar in the main living area, food or coffee in the kitchen, television, video and stereo in another smaller living room. He would be back, he said, as soon as possible.

'Be careful, Antonio,' were her last words.

His parting smile didn't seem to soothe her anxious face. But he couldn't let her natural female tendency for taking the line of least resistance sway him from doing what had to be done.

For a while Antonio thought Waltham *wasn't* home. But he answered his doorbell at long last, the considerable delay explained by his semi-naked state and frustrated expression. His chest and feet were bare, his trousers hanging around his hips, the zipper gaping. His lack of underwear was disgustingly obvious.

'Who the hell—?' he began aggressively, then stopped. 'Oh, it's you! Tony, isn't it?'

'Antonio,' came the cold correction. 'Antonio Scarlatti.'

'Really? You don't sound Italian.' Waltham started

doing up his trousers. 'Sorry about this. I was in the middle of something.' And, zipping up his fly with a pretty risky flourish, he threw Antonio one of those conspiratorial man-to-man grins.

Antonio just stared at him, his emotions wavering between distaste and disbelief. How could Paige have been taken in by this womanising creep, even for a moment?

The stockbroker wasn't at all fazed by Antonio's chilly expression, his own face still smirking. 'Is there something I can help you with, Tony? A cup of sugar? Packet of condoms?'

'I can't imagine you'd have any left,' Antonio drawled icily, and the man's smile finally began to fade.

'Honey, who is it?' A female voice drifted from the depths of the apartment. 'I'm getting cold in here. If you're much longer, I'm going to have to put some clothes on.'

'I'll just be a moment or two, sweetheart,' Waltham called over his shoulder. 'Go pop in the spa and keep it warm for me.'

Antonio's top lip curled with contempt at the sound of the female's empty-headed giggle. The stockbroker began eyeing his visitor with a more thoughtful expression. 'I take it this is not a social call?'

'You take it correctly,' Antonio returned. 'I've come to collect Miss Fortune's clothes.'

'Miss Fortune?' the creep repeated, frowning his confusion.

Antonio's temper was starting to seriously fray. The louse didn't even know Paige's surname.

'The lady's first name is Paige,' came his frosty elaboration. 'But you probably called her honey. Or sweetheart. Or babe.'

Now he got some reaction. Waltham's face darkened,

then tightened. 'Oh, I see. She ran along to you, did she? Probably told you a whole lot of bull about how I beat her up. Hell, it was only a little slap. If it had been any other guy she'd have gotten a lot more than that! Look, man, don't be fooled by the likes of her. She's nothing but a cheap, gold-digging little slut. And frigid to boot.'

Antonio tried not to look startled at this last highly unexpected announcement.

'Not that you would ever guess by looking at her,' Waltham raved on. 'That hot-looking body of hers promises more moves than a chess champion. I spent a damned fortune on taking her to the best restaurants and shows in town. But would she put out afterwards? Not even remotely! At first she said it was too soon, and then she said she just couldn't sleep with a man who didn't love her. She made me so crazy I told her I loved her. I even asked her to move in with me, to prove it. Which, of course, was her plan: to move in with some rich mug so she could claim half of everything they own. Usually I'm too smart for that caper, but I was so frustrated I wasn't thinking straight.

'I wouldn't have minded if she'd been good in bed, but, hell, anyone would think she was a virgin the way she carried on, crying afterwards and then saying she didn't want to do it again. I thought a bit of oral would get her going, but oh, no, she wouldn't have a bar of that, either. It was about then that I lost it and hit her. The silly little cow ran into the bathroom and locked herself in. She was in there so long I had a few drinks, then eventually passed out on the bed. I guess it was while I was asleep that she let herself out and went along to your place.'

Antonio was having difficulty keeping his hands off

the bastard. 'She didn't come along to my place,' he bit out.

'Oh? What happened, then? Did you run into her in the lift, was that it? Well, whatever, just watch it, buddy. She's bad news. A fruit loop. Toss her out before you get caught in the same trap I did. Meanwhile, don't believe a word she says about what happened last night.'

'The bruise on her face rather speaks for itself, don't you think?' Antonio said with cold fury. 'As for Miss Fortune being a gold-digging slut, I don't think what you described to me just now are the actions of a slut. Sluts, I've found, have no aversion to giving men like you whatever you want. As for her being a gold-digger, I would imagine most people would consider *you* the gold-digger for pursuing *her*.'

'Huh? What in hell are you talking about? The girl hasn't got a dime. She hasn't even got a job at the moment!'

'Paige might not personally have any money. But her father could buy your pathetic little stockbroking firm several times over without missing the money. Since Paige is Conrad Fortune's only child and heiress, some people might think she's a very desirable catch, whether she's good in bed or not!'

Antonio rather liked seeing Waltham's mouth flap open like a floundering fish.

'I gather you've heard of Conrad Fortune of Fortune Productions? Their television programmes win awards all over the world every year.'

The four-letter expletive which fell from those flapping lips expressed the stockbroker's situation pretty well, Antonio thought with savage satisfaction.

'I happen to be in Mr Fortune's employ,' he went on mercilessly. 'I see to his security and other personal needs. Italians are, by tradition, very good bodyguards. They don't shirk from doing what other men find...irksome.'

Antonio let his words sink in, with their implied threat. He gave private thanks to all those films which had painted every second Italian male—especially ones dressed in black—as potential killers.

'Recently, Mr Fortune gave me a different brief,' he continued, in the classically emotionless monotone of a movieland Mafia assassin. 'His daughter. I was charged with seeing no harm comes to her. So you see, Jed, I was concerned when it came to my attention that you'd raised your hand to her, then threatened her further.'

Antonio didn't know that Waltham *had* threatened Paige further, but it seemed likely, given her fear.

Waltham had gone a sickly ashen colour.

'You are fortunate that Miss Fortune wants your miserable hide spared. All she asks is the return of her clothes. So if you could get them, please, I'll be on my way.'

Now Waltham went dead white. 'I...I can't get her clothes.'

'Why not?'

'I...um...I burnt them,' he muttered, in the lowest of voices.

'You...burnt...them.'

'Look, when I woke up to find her gone, naturally I was angry,' he tried to explain.

'Naturally?' Antonio repeated coldly.

Waltham suddenly found some spirit. 'Damn it all, what did she expect? That I would calmly take what she dished out? I wanted to teach her a lesson. I'm a man, not a mouse!'

'I agree that you're not a mouse. But you're not a

man either. You're a louse! And it's *you* who's going to be taught the lesson.' The back of Antonio's left hand swiped hard across Waltham's face before the other man could even blink, snapping his head round as the blow landed forcibly on his cheekbone, pretty well in the same place Paige had been struck.

Antonio had no intention of leaving it at that. Taking the stunned man by the shoulders, he let his knee come up between Waltham's legs and crunch into the sleaze-bag's ill-protected equipment. Antonio stepped back and watched him sink to his knees, grasping his genitals as he groaned in agony.

'Don't worry, you'll live,' Antonio told the crouched form at his feet. 'You'll probably even get to be a pathetic lover again. But not tonight, I would imagine. Your ladyfriend will have to keep it warm for a few more days, I would think. Needless to say, if you ever bother Paige again...if you even *speak* to her...either personally or by telephone, you won't get off this lightly a second time. Do you get my drift?'

Waltham managed to nod.

'Smart man,' Antonio said, and walked off.

CHAPTER SEVEN

PAIGE couldn't settle to doing anything Antonio had suggested. Television was beyond her powers of concentration at that moment. She'd never been much of a drinker. And eating was the last thing she could manage. The revolving in her stomach would have rivalled that of a tumbledrier.

She paced up and down the spacious room, oblivious and uncaring of its luxury, her anxiety increasing with each passing minute. Logic suggested it would take Jed time to pack her clothes, but logic was not as strong as the intuitive feeling that something else was going on in the apartment next door besides clothes-packing. Her ears strained to detect any sounds of scuffling or shouting through the walls, but of course million-dollar penthouses were well insulated.

Agitated beyond belief, Paige found herself eventually making her way through the huge sliding glass doors and standing on the equally huge balcony. Again she strained to hear sounds, but nothing came to her ears but the faint sound of music from one of the opened windows below. Sighing her frustration, she leant against the curved steel railing and let the fresh sea breeze blow the heat from her face.

Distraction came in the form of the view of Sydney Harbour. It was magnificent, and very different from that at her own home, which was understandable. The two residences were on opposite sides of Port Jackson, for starters, and opposite sides of the bridge. Antonio's penthouse was also much higher, so that a larger body of water plus the whole of the inner city area was set out before her in one vast, hundred-and-eighty-degree panorama.

At that hour, and with the night sky perfectly clear of cloud, it was a sight to behold. The stars competed with the city lights to create a fairyland carpet out of the black waters of the harbour, a perfect foil for the bridge and the tall buildings beyond. In the distance, Darling Harbour glowed. No doubt its brand-new glitzy casino still buzzed with tourists and compulsive gamblers, but the rest of the city was pretty quiet. It was Monday night, after all, and those balmy summer evenings which brought Sydneysiders out onto the harbour in droves were still a few weeks off.

Paige shivered as a swirl of much stronger wind brought her out in goosebumps. Truly, it was too cool to be comfortable out here, and she turned to go inside. So much for Antonio's suggestion that they sit out on his balcony sipping coffee. He must have known it was out of the question. Which meant he'd probably never intended to bother with supper at all. Till this awkward business with Jed had cropped up, it probably would have been straight to the bedroom.

And she would have been with him all the way!

The thought annoyed her, and she slammed the glass door behind her. Why on earth was the infernal man taking so long?

The need for further distraction drove her to look around the place. Frankly, she was surprised and impressed. Although identical in floor-plan to Jed's penthouse, Antonio's was furnished in a more sophisticated and elegant style. The floors went from a grey granite in the foyer and hallways to a deep burgundy carpet in the living rooms, the furniture a mixture of lacquered black wood and the coolest of cream leathers.

Jed's place was over the top, with lots of dark studded leather, animal print furnishings and mirrors. Oh, yes, Jed liked mirrors!

Each place reflected the personality of its owner, Paige began to appreciate. Jed was a show pony, who needed pseudo-macho accessories to boost his self-image. Antonio didn't. His natural class and taste shone through in the things he'd chosen to surround himself with. This was the home of a man who knew what he was, and what he wanted out of life.

Antonio had obviously done very well for himself over the years, Paige realised as she wandered over to stare through the glass wall at the city skyline once more. A million-dollar view to go with the million-dollar penthouse. That Jag he'd been driving tonight wasn't cheap, either. And his clothes spoke for themselves. Still, her father was no fool. He would be paying Antonio a huge package to make sure no other company head-hunted him.

And, of course, Antonio had no dependants to drain away his finances. No doubt he meant to keep it that way, too. If a man meant to marry and have children he didn't leave it this late to start. Not that Paige knew exactly how old he was. But he had to be in his mid-thirties.

The sound of a key rattling in the front door lock propelled Paige back to the moment at hand and over to the foyer, her heart pounding as Antonio came in. Frantic blue eyes searched his face and hands for any evidence of a scuffle.

But there wasn't any.

Besides being unmarked, his hands were also empty.

'Jed wasn't in?' she asked, perplexed over what could have taken him so long if he hadn't been fighting or gathering up her clothes.

Antonio's smile was wry. 'He was in all right.'

'Oh? He wouldn't give you my clothes, then?'

'He *couldn't* give me your clothes.'

'Oh, my God, what did you do to him?' Paige burst out, frantic that Antonio might have done something really stupid. There was a wild glitter in his eyes which worried the life out of her.

'Nothing,' he denied, and, taking her arm, steered her back into the living room. 'Nothing much, anyway,' he muttered darkly.

'I think I need a drink,' he announced, and, leaving her in the middle of the room, he stalked over to the black-lacquered bar in the corner and poured himself a large whisky. 'You want something?'

'No, thanks. And what do you mean by *nothing much*?'

She watched agitatedly while Antonio took a deep swallow of whisky, then smiled a very rueful little smile. 'Let's say he'll be sporting a bruise bigger than yours tomorrow. And he won't be in a hurry to service the dolly-bird he had stashed in his bedroom. Other than that, he's fine.'

Paige didn't know whether to shout hooray or to cry. In the end, her dismay overrode her satisfaction that Antonio had indeed pulverised the man. 'Jed had a...a woman with him?' she choked out.

'Why do you think I hit him?'

Paige did not know what to say. Or think. She just stood there, her head and shoulders sagging. What a fool she'd been to have felt guilty over Jed even for a moment. His anger last night had not been the result of a broken heart, but a bruised ego.

'He couldn't give me your clothes,' Antonio added. 'Because he'd burnt them.'

'*Burnt* them!' she exclaimed, both startled and shocked. 'Why would he do such a terrible thing?'

'Men like him don't take rejection well,' Antonio stated drily. 'Not many men do, actually. I would say, when he woke and found out you were gone, he had to have something to destroy. Since you were no longer there in person, your clothes were his only option. After that, he went out and found another woman to bolster up his poor, pathetic male ego. He didn't love you, Paige. He *never* loved you.'

Paige could see that now. But it was still an upsetting situation. 'God, I'm an idiot,' she cried, and buried her face in her hands. Tears welled up in her eyes, tears of despair and self-pity. Her father was right about her. She had no idea about men. Jed had fooled her far too easily. Some smooth flattery. Some clever lies. And she'd simply believed him.

She shuddered at her gullibility.

Antonio's taking her gently into his arms seemed so natural, yet it brought a fresh well of emotion flooding her heart, and her eyes. With a strangled sob, she laid her head against his chest, tears spilling down her face.

'Poor Paige,' he crooned as he held her to him, one hand firmly around her waist, the other stroking her hair down her back.

Poor Paige indeed, she had to concede as she wept. Poor, silly, stupid Paige!

She'd actually thought she'd taken her life in hand this year. She'd done that course, got herself a new job, a new wardrobe *and*, she'd mistakenly thought, a new man, to banish Antonio from her mind and heart for ever.

Well, her new job was gone. So was her new man. Even her nice new clothes!

And now she was back, living at her despised home, and loving Antonio more than ever!

Her thoughts gradually brought her back to the reality of that very moment, which was that she was actually in Antonio's arms, and he was holding her to him very, very closely. So closely that she could feel his heartbeat under the palms of her hands, and a telling hardness pressing against her stomach.

This was what she'd been waiting for all her life, wasn't it? *Wasn't it?*

Her tears dried as the heat in her body rose, her own heart quickening. Her weeping stopped, and a tense silence gradually filled the air. Antonio's hand stilled on her back. She felt his pulse-rate pick up speed.

'I think, perhaps,' he said thickly, 'that I should take you home.' And he pushed her away to arm's length.

Paige's head lifted, her eyes wide upon his.

'You're upset,' he ground out, his own eyes like black coals upon hers.

If he'd looked at her with pity, she might have fled. But he didn't. His eyes reflected a passion which was intoxicating in its intensity.

'But I don't *want* to go home,' she told him huskily, and a storm of indecision filled his face.

'I doubt you have any idea what you want, Paige. You never have.'

'There's one thing I've always wanted, Antonio,' she insisted on a raw whisper. 'And that's you...'

'Like you thought you wanted Waltham?'

'I *never* wanted Jed the way I've always wanted you.'

His hands lifted from her shoulders to take her face and tip it upwards. 'Don't expect me to tell you I love you,' he said darkly, his impassioned gaze lancing hers.

'I don't,' she managed to say quite coolly, even though she was trembling inside.

'You told Waltham you only slept with men who loved you. Which was why he said he did.'

Paige was taken aback that Jed would admit such a thing, till she accepted that Antonio might have coerced the information out of him. 'What else did he tell you?'

'That last night was the first time you'd had sex together. Was that true?'

'Yes.'

'Did he use protection?'

'Yes.'

'Have all your other lovers always used protection?'

'What? Oh…oh, yes. Always.' Brad had been very careful about that.

'Good.'

His mouth began to descend, stopping only millimetres from hers. 'Once I kiss you,' he warned, 'there'll be no going back.'

'I won't want to go back.'

'I was talking to myself, Paige,' he muttered. 'Not you.' And his mouth closed the gap.

Antonio fought a deep self-disgust as he started to kiss her. He knew what he was doing was wrong. On all counts. Paige might sound sure about this, but she had to be especially vulnerable at this moment, distressed over what had happened the night before, and now tonight. Her confidence as a woman would be down, her self-esteem shaky. The classic scenario for a rebound affair. The perfect set-up for him to sweep her off her feet before she had time to think too clearly.

Her declaration that she'd always wanted him didn't mitigate Antonio's guilt. If anything, it made it worse, knowing he was taking advantage of that old teenage crush of hers even more cruelly than if he'd done so when she'd been seventeen.

His conscience demanded he not do this. His own self-respect demanded he tell Conrad to shove his black-mailing bargain and stick his job. He'd survive without Fortune Productions!

But would he survive without making love to Paige?

The chemistry which had always sparked between them was much stronger tonight, and dangerously out of hand. With her lips already softened and parting under his, Antonio's conscience was easily ignored, his earlier anger at being manipulated by Conrad totally abandoned. He no longer cared about anything but kissing the beautiful girl in his arms.

As his tongue dipped deep into her mouth, and she moaned softly, his last rational thought was to wonder if he had any condoms anywhere in the place. But then she moaned a second time, and that thought too was consigned to the same place as his conscience.

Paige's hands slid up his chest and around his neck, clasping her to him lest he somehow dematerialise.

'Antonio,' she whispered once, when his mouth lifted briefly. But then he was back, kissing her again, taking her breath away, making her see just why she'd waited so long, and why she hadn't been able to love any other man. She'd thought Jed would be an experienced and ardent lover, able to push Antonio out of her mind. Instead, he'd been quick, and crude. She'd hated every

second of their brief coupling, then shuddered with revulsion when he'd tried more intimate things with her
afterwards.

But when Antonio's mouth moved hotly and hungrily
over hers a wildly uninhibited passion began to burn
through her body, a passion which *demanded* intimacies.
She could not wait to touch him all over, to stroke his
skin and kiss his most private places. In turn, she wanted
his hands on her, stripping away all her clothes, explor-
ing every inch of her naked flesh, searching out every
forbidden erotic zone. Her body was his to enjoy and to
use. She would give it to him.

Willingly.

Wantonly.

Lovingly.

They were both breathless by the time his hands fell
to her clothes. Paige helped him, undoing the small
pearly buttons between her breasts when he had trouble,
tugging the silky garment back off her shoulders and
letting it flutter to the floor, leaving her naked to the
waist.

Touch me, she begged him silently. Touch *them*. Oh,
please, Antonio. Please.

Antonio's breath sucked in sharply at the sight of Paige's
magnificent breasts, with their lush fullness and rose-
tipped peaks. They stood out in their arousal, taut and
tempting. But he didn't touch them, forcing himself to
wait till she was totally naked before him.

'Take off the rest,' he ordered thickly, and after the
briefest hesitation she obeyed him, swiftly, completely.
Dear God, what that did to him, seeing her eager com-
pliance to his wishes, watching her quite stunning beauty
unfold before his eyes.

She was even more lovely than he'd imagined. A golden goddess. A temptress beyond description.

Paige's head swam as she stood there before him, watching his smouldering gaze move slowly over her totally nude body. She could not have been more turned on if he was actually touching her. Her stomach tightened. Her breasts swelled. Her thighs quivered.

'Don't move,' he ordered, and set to slowly undressing himself in front of her.

First his jacket. Then his top. Both discarded without a care. His eyes were solely on her, eating her up, telling her with every searing glance that he wanted her more than any man had ever wanted her.

His shoes were kicked off, his socks soon after. And then it was down to the nitty-gritty. His trousers and his underpants. Her mouth dried as he dropped the first, then stepped out of the second.

Her breath caught in her throat. Oh, yes…he wanted her more than any man had ever wanted her!

Paige stared down at him, then up into his face, and knew she was about to experience something very different from anything she'd ever experienced before. This would be nothing like Brad's gentle, easy-going style of lovemaking, or Jed's ghastly wham-bam-thank-you-ma'am brand of sex.

'Come here,' he commanded.

She felt as if she was in slow motion as she moved back into his arms, her lips gasping open at the feel of their naked bodies meeting, then melting together. She lifted her face to be kissed, but he didn't kiss her, just stared deep into her wide, dilated eyes.

'You do realise,' he warned in a strangled voice, 'that I can't wait a moment longer.'

'Neither can I,' she heard herself say, and he made a sound she would always remember. A raw, guttural groan which encapsulated everything and nothing of what she'd hoped he'd one day feel for her. Her own feelings were indescribable, her love for him momentarily abandoned in favour of sheer lust. She could never have dreamt of such urgency, or such a need. She simply *had* to have Antonio inside her, had to feel his flesh filling hers, stamping her body with his unique brand of sexuality.

'Just do it, Antonio,' she urged wildly. 'Do it!'

With another of those tortured groans, he pushed her legs apart and penetrated her then and there, filling her with a savage upward thrust which brought a stunned cry to her lips. She'd known he would be a passionate and primitive lover, known he would take her breath away. What she hadn't known was that she would thrill to such caveman treatment. When his large hands cupped her buttocks and hoisted her up off the floor she buried her face into his neck lest he see what was in her eyes.

But hiding her face from him was impossible when he carried her over and tipped her back across the high, wide leather arm of the sofa in the centre of the room. Her mouth opened on a gasp as her head and shoulders sank into the squashy cushions, her hair flying everywhere, her arms flopping up above her head. Her sex, however, remained firmly fused with Antonio's.

Stunned, she stared up at him from the depths of the sofa. She'd never experienced or imagined such a position. Yet it was surprisingly comfortable, especially after her legs snaked around his waist, her ankles linking. Her hips were well supported by the soft leather arm, her buttocks firmly clasped in Antonio's strong male hands.

It was also an incredibly erotic position, with their bodies so explicitly displayed for each other's eyes.

Paige thought Antonio looked magnificent, standing there with his long legs braced solidly apart, his broad shoulders and muscular arms having no trouble holding her to him like that. The years hadn't brought any flab to his stomach, though his tan was possibly more due to his Latin genes than time spent in the sun. His body hair seemed darker and more menacing than she remembered, or maybe that was because she hadn't seen that part which was now totally exposed, and closest to her wide-eyed gaze.

Dressed, Antonio always looked a handsome and elegant man. Nude, he was the primitive lover Paige had always pictured, and wanted.

His glittering black eyes took in every inch of her body with a slow and decidedly thorough survey, bringing a flush of heat to her cheeks and a squirming feeling to the pit of her stomach. Under his gaze her parched lips fell further apart, her nipples peaked harder, her belly tightened.

When his eyes reached that part of her which was as one with his he began to move, and to move *her*, his hands pulling her hard against him with each thrust of his hips.

'Oh, God,' she moaned, and simply had to close her eyes, her head twisting to one side, her helpless hands finding and grasping a cushion with frantic opening and closing movements of her fingers. It was impossible to think of anything but what he was doing to her body. How *he* felt. How *she* felt.

The blood was roaring in her head. Her heart was going faster and faster. Everything was spinning way, way out of control.

And just when Paige began to panic she shattered around him, crying out his name, her tortured face and wildly spasming body bringing hot tears to her eyes. For this was even worse than she'd feared. The pleasure. And the pain.

Because Antonio did not love her. He would *never* love her.

Just like Jed.

CHAPTER EIGHT

ANTONIO was stunned by the power of her orgasm, and the rush of elation it evoked within him.

Strange...he'd never been that kind of man before, whose ego needed stroking by the woman he was with. He'd never felt the urge to prove himself a greater lover than her last, never strived to impress in bed so that his partner thought he was the best thing since Casanova.

But it seemed that with Paige he *was*. His dark triumph at being able to give her such pleasure was only exceeded by the pleasure *he* was finding in *her* body. Maybe his memory was playing tricks on him, but he couldn't remember it feeling this good, even with Lauren. Or this wild!

Antonio had to admit that Conrad's daughter had been his sexual nemesis for a long time. But especially now, with her violent climax propelling him towards a climax of his own which was as compellingly irresistible as it was highly risky.

For he wasn't wearing a condom.

He'd meant to go and get one. There were surely some in his bathroom or in his bedside table drawer. Antonio always believed in being prepared.

But things had got out of hand. When she'd urged him to just do it, he'd totally lost his head.

Of course, he could still withdraw and get one.

Or he could just withdraw.

But he wasn't going to, was he?

Not because he was trying to get her pregnant.

Frankly, the thought of Paige conceiving would complicate things. How could he divorce the mother of his child?

The truth was he didn't want anything between his flesh and hers when he came. He wanted to keep feeling the heat of her, the tightness, the wetness. And he wanted to go on experiencing the indescribable ecstasy of what he was feeling at that moment.

Her contractions showed absolutely no sign of abating. It was unbelievable! Unbearable! If only he could last for ever. But then she called out his name again, and arched her back in one long, voluptuous movement, shifting the angle of her body, breaking what little was left of his control.

He came with a lightning flash of sensation, his cry as loud as a thunderclap. His fingers were digging into her flesh and his thighs trembling uncontrollably when the sudden urge for closer contact sent him bending over to scoop her up from the depths of the sofa, holding her tight against him while he shuddered deep within her.

At first she just clung to him, but then she started to cry, with deep, gasping sobs.

It rocked him, that gut-wrenching sobbing. Rocked and rattled him. Waltham had said something about her crying with him afterwards.

But surely this wasn't the same kind of crying! This couldn't be dismay or disappointment, or, God forbid, disgust. It had to be a reaction to the intensity of her release. He'd heard of such things happening, though hadn't come across it before.

He wanted to comfort her, to say something, *anything* to stop her heartbreaking weeping.

'Hush, honey, hush,' he found himself saying, his hands shaking slightly as they stroked her hair down her back. 'It's all right, Paige. It's all right. Please don't cry. Please, sweetheart…don't.'

She gradually stopped, and with one last hiccuping sob lifted luminescent blue eyes to his. They searched his face, looking for…what? he wondered.

And then she murmured something which rocked him even more than her crying.

'Make love to me, Antonio.'

He stared down at her. What did she think he'd *been* doing?

And then the penny dropped. The reason for the weeping. The disillusionment with Jed, and all her other lovers. Her distress over what had just happened between them. She didn't want just sex. She wanted love. She didn't want harsh reality. She wanted romance. It was as Conrad had said.

Just tell her you love her, said a voice in Antonio's head, and she'll be putty in your hands. Consolidate your declaration with some truly tender lovemaking, and marriage will be just around the corner.

He instinctively recoiled from such a cruel deception. She deserved better than a husband who didn't really love her, who would manipulate her like that. If he cared about her at all he would take her home right now and walk out of her life for ever.

And leave her for Brock Masters? His pragmatic side piped up again. Throw away everything you've worked for as well?

And what about your child? another voice inserted savagely. The one who might have been conceived here tonight? Who can say what Paige might do if she finds herself pregnant? Could you live with yourself if she does what Lauren did, not out of greed, but despair? You can see how vulnerable she is, man. Just *look* at her!

A whole host of emotions tore through Antonio. And while he tried to tell himself there were mitigating circumstances for what he'd done tonight, and what he was about to do, his main feeling was a raging guilt.

Oh, Paige, Paige, he agonised as he bent to cover her lovely mouth with his. Forgive me…

Paige could not believe the gentleness of his kiss. Or the way he looked down at her afterwards. With such sweet tenderness.

It brought tears to her eyes, and to her soul. Her parched, love-starved soul.

'Antonio,' she murmured, and held her hand against his cheek.

He didn't say a word as he carried her into the darkened bedroom; nor when he drew her down with him onto the huge bed; nor when he started making love to her again.

No matter. She didn't want words at that moment. Words would have spoiled the fantasy, the fantasy that Antonio loved her.

In the security of her silent dreamworld Paige could believe anything she chose. And she chose to believe there was more to Antonio's lovemaking than lust this time. It was there in the softness of his mouth and the gentleness of his touch. But most of all it was in the swift readiness of his body to give her pleasure and satisfaction once more.

No man, Paige enjoyed deluding herself, could want her again so quickly, unless she meant more to him than a one-night stand.

Not since her days at school had she enjoyed one of her fantasies so much, letting reality slip away as she sighed beneath her pretend love, sighed, then groaned, then gasped, her hips lifting to meet Antonio's as they came together one more amazing and marvellous time.

It was only afterwards, while Paige held him in her arms and felt him slip away into sleep, that reality re-surfaced and she knew she could never bear to do this again.

Once was enough.

Once she could live with.

Twice would surely destroy her.

The only plus from tonight was that there was no pos-sibility of a pregnancy to compound her stupidity. She'd started taking the pill a couple of years ago, after a near-date-rape scare one night, at the suggestion of a kindly doctor who'd said girls these days were always at risk, with sexual assault so rampant. Of course, she knew the pill wouldn't protect her from AIDS or other STDs. And once or twice she'd contemplated stopping. She was glad now that she hadn't.

Lord knows what Antonio had been thinking, how-ever, when he'd gone ahead without protection. Had he presumed she was using some form of protection? Or did he believe she would think nothing of having an abortion if she fell pregnant?

She hated to think he would think that badly of her. Still, she supposed the responsibility for what had hap-pened *was* mainly hers. *She'd* been the one to push the issue. She'd been the one who'd refused to go home, who'd told him to just do it, asked him to do it again. Fair enough if he assumed the worst.

He probably thought she was a big tart.

Not that it really mattered what he thought of her. All that mattered was that she extricate herself from his life as quickly as possible. Knowing men, he would probably want to keep her on tap for the rest of his fortnight's holiday. Heck, why not? He probably thought she was good for every which way he might like his sex. Kinky. Straight. Wild. Warm. He must have thought he'd won the sexual lottery!

Paige bit her bottom lip to stop herself from crying again, steeling herself inside with tough thoughts. She'd shed enough tears tonight. Frankly, she'd shed enough tears over Antonio to last a lifetime! Enough was enough. Time to take control of her wayward heart and weak flesh. Time to show him who was boss of her life.

She really could not allow herself to continue being a victim of her futile feelings.

She had to make a stand!

Sliding out from under him, she slipped from the bed, stopping only long enough to pick up the bottom of the quilt and throw it over his naked body. She could not bear to look at him like that, or to look at him at all for that matter. Not right now. Shortly, perhaps, when she'd washed the smell of him from her body and put something on to cover the evidence of his lovemaking. Maybe then she would be able to face him.

Antonio woke to a shake of his shoulder. He blinked a couple of times into the overhead light before focusing on the figure beside the bed.

Paige, he finally realised. Fully dressed. And with a slightly impatient expression on her face.

'Sorry to wake you,' she said briskly. 'But I really must be going home, and I didn't bring any money with me.'

Antonio's brain was still fuzzy from sleep. 'What do you need money for?'

'For a taxi, silly. You don't think I expect you to get up and drive me home, do you? You must be wrecked after your long day. Not to mention your pretty exhausting night.

'Not that I'm not grateful, mind,' she added, bending and giving him a peck on his startled mouth. 'You're as fantastic in bed as I always thought you'd be. And, frankly, after Jed, I needed my faith in male virility restored a little. But let's be honest, Antonio, you're not looking for a permanent female to share your life, whereas I'm reaching the stage where real commitment is what I'm looking for. Actually, one-night stands never did appeal to me. Why do you think I always lived with my boyfriends?'

She batted her eyelashes at him and smiled a sickly sweet smile. 'So, darling, as much as I fancy you enormously, I think we'll leave it right here. Oh, by the way, if you're worried there's a chance a little Scarlatti heir might have been produced tonight, then don't be. I'm on the pill. Not that I usually tell a man that. But you can know now that our sexual relationship is over.'

Antonio could find nothing to say to her. He supposed he should have felt relieved about the pill business. But he wasn't. Frankly, he was too taken aback by this whole unexpected turn of events to assemble his emotions—and thoughts—properly. Only one fact was sinking in, which was that despite Paige's verbal flattery over his performance in bed she wasn't nearly as vulnerable to him as he'd thought, or hoped.

'We really were both very silly tonight, weren't we?' she went on, in that faintly patronising tone. 'I guess I was upset over Jed, and you...well perhaps you've been working too hard, Antonio, and not getting enough regular sex. What you need is some desperate divorcee to satisfy your needs over the next fortnight, and I'll look for someone a little more suited to *my* needs. You get my drift?'

Antonio got her drift all right. Desperate divorcee indeed!

And there he'd been earlier, worrying about taking advantage of the girl, thinking she was a push-over. She was about as much of a push-over as her father!

But she'd shown her hand to him in more ways than one tonight. For one thing she wasn't in any way frigid, as Waltham had implied. That idiot must have been pretty terrible in bed. Paige liked her sex and she liked it a lot. She just preferred it with commitment.

Commitment, he mused, was the name of the game. Not love, so much. Or even romance.

Now commitment he could handle. Commitment he was familiar with. He'd been committed to Fortune Productions for years. All he had to do was do what he did at work when he went after a contract or a deal. Devote every breathing, waking moment to the challenge, and never take no for an answer!

'You don't *have* to go home, do you?' he said softly, and sat up, the quilt falling off his naked shoulders.

She turned away from him and stood up, laughing. 'Oh, yes, I do. No way am I going to waltz up home tomorrow morning after staying out all night with you, Antonio. A girl has her pride.'

'Pride?'

'Everyone around Fortune Hall knows you're the love 'em and leave 'em type. I have no intention of being added to your list of idle conquests. Bad enough that I once made a fool of myself over you. I don't intend to repeat the performance, or give Evelyn any opportunity to sneer down her nose at me. Not to mention my father! Good grief, the thought is too horrible for words. So you can either hop up and drive me home, or lend me some money for a taxi. It doesn't matter to me either way.'

Oh, it didn't, did it? Antonio began to fume. We'll just see about that, Miss Love 'em and Leave 'em yourself! I've got news for you. You won't be loving and leaving *me*, honey. You're going to be my wife, whether you want to be or not!

'I wouldn't dream of sending you home in a taxi,' he said with a smooth smile, and, throwing off the quilt, bounced naked from the bed. 'Just give me a minute...'

Paige groaned as she watched his gorgeous behind disappear into the *en suite* bathroom. That was *not* a sight which reinforced her decision to have done with the infernal man once and for all!

On top of that, Antonio himself didn't seem to want to leave things between them at a one-nighter. If he had, he would have taken up her suggestion of a taxi. He would not be rushing to escort her home.

Antonio had seemed genuinely taken aback by her decision not to see him again. No doubt he wasn't used to such rash treatment from women he'd just brought to rapture in his bed. Paige could not imagine many of his sexual partners not lining up eagerly for seconds. Or thirds.

But she wasn't one of his casual sexual partners, was she? She *loved* the man.

No! She would *not* weaken. She'd spoken her mind to him—and, in essence, it was the truth. She *did* want commitment. She'd had enough of loneliness, and heartache. She was fed up to her eye-teeth with men asking her out, then expecting her to jump into bed the very first night. She wanted someone who wanted what she wanted. She wanted someone whom she could love, and who would love her back. She wanted…the impossible. She sighed.

The bathroom door opened and out strode Antonio, all wet and glistening from the shower, his still naked body just barely decent with a towel slung round his hips.

Paige tried not to look anything but amused. 'You going to drive me home like that, Antonio?'

His smile was wickedly attractive, and totally disarming. 'Would you like me to?'

Her face grew hot at the thought. 'Don't be ridiculous!' she snapped.

He shrugged. 'I guess I'll have to get dressed, then.' And he headed for the living room.

Paige made the mistake of following him and watching while he discarded the towel right in front of her and began to dress with irritating slowness, starting with his underpants and trousers. Once they were thankfully in place, he actually sat down on the sofa where he'd made love to her—if you could call that torrid encounter making love!—and took his time putting on his shoes and socks.

Such a sight and setting was not conducive to pure thoughts and brave resolves. Paige stared at Antonio's semi-naked body and started thinking of all the things she'd wanted to do with the man and hadn't. She hadn't even touched him all over. It had been all Antonio directing everything. Antonio doing the kissing and the caressing. Antonio choosing the positions.

A pity, Paige thought regretfully.

She'd once had this fantasy of giving a completely nude Antonio a long, sensual massage. She would relax him totally with the skill of her hands first, then slowly arouse him with her mouth till he was in a state of the most acute arousal. Only when he begged her would she slide over and down onto his aching flesh, where she—

'I'm ready,' Antonio drawled, and Paige was dragged back to reality, her mouth snapping shut with a nasty little lurch in her stomach.

For Antonio was watching her closely, and with a slightly smug smile. Panic propelled her madly racing heart into momentary arrest. What had he seen just now? What had he guessed? Had he been aware of her staring at him as he dressed? Had he seen the lust in her glazed eyes?

Yes, of course he had! *He* might be an expert at wearing a poker face, but she wasn't quite so skilful over hiding her feelings. He must have felt the hunger in her glued gaze, then recognised the reason behind her faraway expression, her parted lips, her flushed cheeks.

Somehow, she managed to school her face into a casual expression, but the damage had been done. Still, if she were brutally honest with herself, the damage had been done earlier tonight, when she'd responded to him with such abandon, then begged him for more.

'Fine,' she said crisply. 'Let's go.'

She stalked off ahead of him towards the door, then stood at a distance in the corridor while he locked up. But Antonio was not to be so easily denied. The moment they were alone together in the lift his hand found hers, his fingers sliding between hers, then curling them over.

Her stomach curled over as well.

The automatic and involuntary response annoyed Paige. But it underlined her vulnerability to the man. Really, this was the last time she could allow herself to be alone with him.

Meanwhile, she had to let him know that she had his measure.

Snatching her hand out of his would have seemed melodramatic, and panicky. So she left it there, pasted a wry little smile on her mouth and threw him a gently mocking glance.

The predatory gleam in his return gaze reaffirmed what she'd already suspected. Antonio wasn't going to give up easily. *He* was the one who wanted more now.

But only for the next fortnight.

Only a fool would think otherwise. Once his two-week break was over he'd be winging his way back to Europe, without Paige just a pleased smile on his hand-some face.

The thought made her doubly determined not to let him seduce her again. She'd wasted enough of her life pining after this man. It was definitely time to move on.

The lift doors opened in the basement and she managed to free her fingers without making a fuss. He didn't appear disconcerted by her distancing herself a little as they walked to the car together, but she was sure she detected a slight stiffening of the muscles in his jawline, and in the set of his broad shoulders.

Antonio's earlier advice, to study his body language, not his face, did not bring Paige any comfort. Somehow, she didn't think her father's right-hand man had reached his present position in the company by being meek and mild, or by turning the other cheek. Although a quiet achiever, he was, nevertheless, an achiever. He would not be overly familiar with experiences such as failure, or rejection. What he wanted, he probably usually got. And that included women.

Paige had no illusions about Antonio in *that* regard. Which meant she had to be extra careful, didn't she?

There would be no accepting any invitation from him, no matter how innocent-sounding it was. Or how desperate she was to get away from her father, or Evelyn, or whatever.

She had to be strong, not weak.

She had to be firm, not foolish.

She had to say *no*!

CHAPTER NINE

'WHAT are you doing tomorrow?'

Paige had been waiting for this, and it came at the first set of lights.

'Today, you mean,' she corrected.

'Don't be pedantic, Paige.'

'I'll be very busy,' she informed him, and he threw her a disbelieving glance.

'Doing what? You're unemployed at the moment.'

'Exactly. And I aim to get *un*-unemployed! Very quickly.'

'But there's not much you can do on a Tuesday. Any phone-in jobs from Saturday's *Herald* will have gone. The rest will require a resumé sent in, which can be done any day this week. The closing date is usually ages after the ad.'

'You've obviously forgotten my telling you, Antonio,' she pointed out firmly, feeling quite proud of herself, 'but I signed up with an agency. They have jobs on their books all the time, especially jobs for temps. If I phone them as soon as they open, I could be at an interview this very afternoon. My only problem is that I don't have any clothes to wear, except what I have on.'

'You don't have any other clothes at *all*?'

'Only what I wore home. A pair of blue jeans, a white shirt and a black jacket.'

'Nothing in your wardrobes at home?'

'A few things left behind from years ago. That's where this outfit came from. But you should see the rest.

Other than the odd bikini, shorts and T-shirt, the rest are dresses bought during my 'crush-on-Antonio' phase. No doubt you won't remember my coming down to dinner in them, but believe me when I tell you they are not dresses you'd wear to an interview. Not unless it's for a job up at the Cross,' she added, with a rueful laugh.

Antonio's laugh was just as rueful. 'Actually, I *do* remember you in a few of those dresses. And I know exactly what you mean. They fuelled a thousand X-rated fantasies for me back then.'

Paige stared helplessly over at him and he laughed again. 'You should see the look on your face. I told you I'd always been attracted to you. Didn't you believe me?'

'In a word? No!'

'Believe me, then,' he stated firmly as the lights turned green and the Jag roared off, heading towards the bridge.

Paige settled into a brooding silence in the passenger seat, angry at being rattled so easily by this declaration. But it had sounded so genuine!

He had to be just flattering her, surely. If he'd always found her so darned attractive, why hadn't he asked her out during any one of her many visits home? His excuse over her tender age had no longer held water then!

She felt Antonio's eyes flick her way as they slowed on their approach to the bridge toll, but she kept her own eyes steadfastly on the road ahead.

'Do you still have that red dress?' he asked. 'The one you wore to last year's Christmas party?'

'What?' Her head whipped round in shock. 'No...no, I don't,' she said sharply.

The irony of it was she'd thrown it in the gardener's

incinerator the following morning, and watched with a perverse satisfaction while it went up in smoke.

Recalling the incident brought some understanding of what Jed had done. There was something darkly cathartic about burning something which shouted failure at you.

'That's a shame,' Antonio said, and leant out to plop a coin in the automatic pay basket.

Her eyes followed, their expression a mixture of curiosity and cynicism. 'Oh? And why's that? It's hardly a suitable outfit for an interview, either.'

He didn't look at her while the electric window slid back up into place and the car moved off again, his attention returning to the road ahead. 'I was thinking you could wear it when I take you to dinner tonight,' he said casually.

Paige had to admire his persistence. But not his presumption. Or his arrogance. 'You'll have to be disappointed, then, won't you? I—'

'No matter,' he broke in, before she could tell him where he could stick his invitation to dinner. 'Wear one of those other little numbers you used to tease the hell out of me with. I distinctly recall a sparkly gold one, which had no back, a microscopic skirt and a halter neckline held together by the most devious, decadent little bow a designer ever created. I used to wonder what would happen if I came up behind you and tugged loose one of those teeny-tiny ties.'

Astonishment that he should recall any of those dresses, let alone one in such detail, sent Paige into a spin.

'So what *would* have happened?' he murmured, and slid those sexy black eyes over to her own startled gaze.

'Or should I just continue to let such a scene live on in my fantasies?'

Paige was totally speechless.

'I've embarrassed you,' he said. 'Sorry. I didn't mean to.'

'No it's all right,' Paige hastened to assure him. 'I'm just surprised, that's all. To be honest, I'm surprised about a lot of things tonight.'

You're not the only one, honey, Antonio thought savagely to himself. What had begun as Conrad's black-mailing bargain this morning had somehow developed into a personal challenge. He no longer cared about being blackmailed into marrying Paige. All he cared about was winning!

Antonio had always been a bit like a dog with a bone whenever someone told him he couldn't do something, or have something. It was a sure way to increase his determination to succeed at whatever project he had in mind, whether it be a business contract or, as in this case, a woman.

And Conrad's daughter was finally and definitely a woman. Quite an impressive woman, really, Antonio had to concede, with a surprisingly strong mind of her own.

He had underestimated her.

As had her father.

But he didn't underestimate her any longer. He understood her a lot better now as well. He appreciated the way her mind worked, not to mention her body.

That was the key to success where Paige was concerned, Antonio believed. That beautiful body of hers, and its uncontrollable cravings.

He'd seen the way she'd looked at him while he

dressed, seen the intensity of her desire smoke up her eyes.

He didn't know if it was him she wanted so much, or simply sex. All he knew was it was a pretty powerful need which had propelled her into his arms tonight, not once, but twice. He'd always suspected she was a hot little number. He just hadn't realised *how* hot.

If only he could get her alone with him again. Not for a night here and there, but for a considerable chunk of time. *Several* days and nights. *Then* she wouldn't be fobbing him off as she had that inadequate idiot, Waltham!

An idea came to Antonio, plus what he hoped was the right approach. At least he didn't have to lie. Or tell her he loved her.

'I don't know about you, Paige,' he said softly, 'but I thought tonight was pretty incredible. I can honestly say that I've never felt like that with any other woman in my life.'

Oh, damn, there it was again! That look! That totally vulnerable, frighteningly fearful, sweetly adoring look! Lord, but it tugged at his heartstrings.

The trouble was, his heartstrings didn't lead to a heart. He didn't *have* a heart. Didn't she know that yet?

He preferred Paige when she was tough, and just a touch cynical. He also preferred her naked and moaning. He definitely preferred her not doing anything to make him feel like a heel!

Paige tried not to react to such an outrageous statement, but it was impossible to stop that flood of fresh yet probably futile hope.

Because he could not mean it, surely. She couldn't have been that special to him, not Antonio, with all his other women.

Big blue eyes searched his darkly handsome face for any sign of sincerity, but only his mouth was smiling. His beautiful black eyes were, if anything, almost cold.

Her heart sank at the reality behind his words. He was just trying to con her back into his bed. Her own eyes grew cold and her laugh was dry. 'More special than the woman you were with at last year's Christmas party?' she scorned lightly. 'The one you were practically ravishing on the terrace?'

She watched his startled expression with a degree of vengeful satisfaction. 'Come now, Antonio,' she flung at him, 'I've heard all those lines before. You'll have to come up with something better than that if you want to go out with me again.'

Like, *I love you, Paige, and I want to marry you!*

'Actually, I've decided I don't want to go out with you again,' he returned coolly, and Paige's heart lurched.

'I want you to go away with me,' he added, and she stopped breathing altogether.

'I've rented this houseboat on the Hawkesbury River for ten days,' he went on, while her head whirled. 'I pick it up at Brooklyn this Wednesday. My plan was to just cruise around, fish, sunbake, read, listen to music. I always need to relax after a few months in that rat-race over in Europe. I was going to go alone...till tonight. Now, I suspect my mind won't rest for thinking about you. As for my body...it hasn't got a chance in Hades of resting, let alone relaxing. It will be suffering an agony of eternal frustration...'

His eyes lanced her with a look which was anything but cold this time. It smouldered and burned its way into every pore in her body, igniting her once more with longing for him.

'I'm not going to make false promises, Paige,' he continued, while she tried not to gape, 'but I too am reaching a stage—and an age—when I'm looking for someone steady in my life. So if you meant what you said about wanting commitment, if you still feel anything for me at all...then come away with me...

'*Please.*'

Was it that fervent *please* which swayed her? Or had she been a goner from the moment he'd looked at her as if she was everything he desired in this world?

Whatever, how could she pass up a chance to make her dreams come true, even if it *was* only a slim chance? Paige wasn't a complete fool. After her experience with Jed, she knew some men would say and do anything sometimes to get a girl into bed.

And to keep her there.

'If I come with you,' she said, 'what will I tell my father?'

'Is that a yes?'

She tried to keep her face nonchalant, knowing men responded better to uncertainty, strange, perverse creatures that they were. 'I guess so. As I said earlier tonight, I've always fancied you. I suspect you could make me fall in love with you, if I gave you the chance,' she added with considerable irony. 'But I'm not making any false promises, either, Antonio. I want more from a relationship than just great sex.'

'But of course,' he replied smoothly. 'As for what your father will say, when have you ever cared about what he thought? Still, if you're worried, don't tell him. Just leave with me on Wednesday while he's at work, and leave a note behind, saying you're going away with a friend for a brief holiday. That way, he won't have to know about us, unless something comes of all this.'

'But what if something does? A relationship with me

might affect your position in the company. Have you thought of that?'

Clearly he hadn't, by the shocked look on his face.

'I'm not sure how or why that would be.'

Paige wished she hadn't brought the subject up now. It might give Antonio second thoughts. But surely he must know how ruthless her father could be sometimes.

'You saw how he was tonight,' she pointed out unhappily. 'He wasn't too thrilled with our going out together. He also might be very annoyed if he thinks we've deceived him. You should know better than anyone that my father is not a man who likes to be crossed. He might take it into his head to fire you, or something horrible like that!'

Antonio's frown cleared, and he slanted her a reassuring smile. 'Don't you worry your pretty little head about my position in the company. I can guarantee your father won't fire me over any relationship I might have with you. In fact I think he'd be pleased as punch to see you with a man who wants more from you than the obvious.'

Her stomach contracted. 'Do you *really* want more from me than that, Antonio?'

'You have no idea how much more, darling Paige,' he murmured, those sexy black eyes of his flicking over her once more.

Her eyes widened while her heart flip-flopped.

Well, how *could* she have any idea? All this was as unexpected as it was beguiling.

Wednesday suddenly seemed an eternity away.

'Do...do you still want to take me to dinner tonight?' she asked breathlessly.

He didn't answer for a few seconds. Perhaps it was

the tricky intersection they were going through at the time, but Paige suspected it wasn't traffic on his mind.

'I think,' he said finally, 'since you're so worried about your father's reaction…we might give dinner tonight a miss.'

'Oh…' She could not keep the disappointment out of her voice, or her face.

'Yes, I feel the same, believe me. But the waiting will make our time together all the better. Be ready for me at nine Wednesday morning.'

His words evoked the perturbingly erotic thought that she would always be ready for him.

'Don't forget,' she said thickly, 'I…I don't have much in the way of clothes.'

'You won't need much. Those casual things you mentioned you had at home should do. The weather forecast is for warm sunny weather for the next few days, but bring your jeans and jacket just in case it turns nasty. What you're wearing would be perfect if we stop off for dinner any night at some riverside restaurant.'

Paige's mind went to that gold lamé dress Antonio seemed to remember so well. Would she dare wear that for him one night? And if she did…what would he do?

Exactly the same as he's planning on doing to you *every* night, darling, came a decidedly cynical voice. That's what this little boat trip is basically all about. Sex. Sex. And more sex. That line about his reaching an age where he's looking for commitment is probably nothing more than exactly that. A line.

And you fell for it, didn't you, you fool.

But it was too late now. She'd said yes. And, if she were honest, wild horses would not stop her going off with Antonio this Wednesday. Her earlier resolve not to ever be alone with him again had been swept away by the slimmest of hopes, and the strongest of desires. The truth was the thought of having him all to herself for ten days in the privacy of a houseboat was just too exciting to resist.

And, who knew? Maybe something *would* come of it. Maybe.

CHAPTER TEN

ANTONIO's bedside phone rang at seven the following morning. It persisted, despite his attempts to ignore it. Only one person, he finally accepted, would be so rude, or so persistent.

He snatched up the receiver and put it to his ear. 'Conrad,' he said firmly, 'I'm on holiday.'

'Only in a manner of speaking,' his boss replied wryly. 'So what happened last night? Evelyn tells me Paige got in very late.'

Antonio bristled. 'Is that one of your housekeeper's duties? Spying for you?'

'She's an employee.'

'Which means she's expected to do your bidding, regardless,' he said sarcastically.

'She's a naturally observant woman.'

Antonio thought of the atmosphere between Paige and the housekeeper last night and found himself very much on Paige's side.

'Was it Evelyn who told Lew about the incident with Paige by the pool all those years ago?' he asked.

'I would imagine so. But what in hell has that got to do with anything?' Conrad snapped. 'I rang up to find out about here and now, not past history. Did you or did you not make love to my daughter last night? Is she or is she not going to marry you?'

'I have no intention of answering either of those questions, Conrad. Do you ask for a blow by blow description of how I go about getting you the best deals for your programmes?'

'Of course not. I know how competent you are at everything you do. I trust you implicitly.'

'Then trust me in this regard. Believe me, when Paige actually agrees to marry me you'll be the first to know.'

'You sound pretty confident she will.'

Antonio was hopeful, but not arrogantly smug. It would be dangerous to presume she was a sure thing. Paige was a far more complex creature than he'd ever imagined.

And far more intriguing.

Frankly, he could not wait for Wednesday to come.

'She's coming away with me tomorrow for a holiday together,' he said a little testily. 'Is that good enough for you?'

'Good God, but you're a fast worker! A holiday together, eh? Where?'

'That's my secret.'

'You like to play a close hand, don't you, Antonio?'

'I like to run my own race, Conrad. And I *don't* like being blackmailed.'

'I'll bet you liked it well enough last night,' his boss chuckled, and suddenly Antonio hated the man.

'That's my private and personal business,' he said frostily. 'Which reminds me. I don't want you making any leading remarks about last night to Paige. Or asking her any awkward questions about me. Ironically, your daughter is worried for my career if we become involved. After your disapproving father act last night, she thought you wouldn't like the idea of our having a relationship.'

'I told you my opposition would work in your favour. Obviously it did.'

'I have no idea if it did or it didn't. I only know that I don't want Paige upset.'

'My God, you really care about her, don't you?'

Antonio almost laughed. Men like Conrad had no conception of what real caring was all about. Real caring was *not* what he was doing with Paige. Though, to be honest, he liked her a darned sight more than her father.

'I'm simply looking after my best interests, Conrad,' he refuted. 'A distressed Paige is not going to make for an amenable companion.'

'Mum's the word, then, my boy.'

'I'm not your boy, Conrad.'

'You're right. You're not. You've always been your own man, Antonio, and I admire that about you. That's why you were my first choice for a son-in-law.'

'Really? Well, with Brock Masters as my understudy, you'd better damned well hope I'm successful!'

'I'm confident you will be.'

'Whether I am or not is entirely in Paige's hands.'

'I doubt that, Antonio. I would think it's very much in *your* hands.' And he hung up.

Antonio felt a moment of sheer fury and frustration before slamming the receiver down as well.

Only then did Evelyn quietly replace her extension, a nasty little smile on her face.

Paige was still sound asleep at eight, when Evelyn went into her room with a breakfast tray. The housekeeper looked down at the girl's exquisitely beautiful profile and felt a jab of jealousy so violent that she was momentarily consumed with the urge to tip the whole tray over her lovely face.

But she kept her temper, and lowered the tray carefully onto the dressing table.

She'd always hated the girl. Hated the beauty she took for granted and the inherited wealth she scorned. Evelyn especially hated the fact Paige didn't seem to care about either of those things.

But the girl cared about Antonio.

Oh, yes…she cared about Antonio very much indeed. She would be devastated when she learnt Antonio had married her not out of love but out of ambition.

And the silly little fool *would* agree to marry him. It was as sure as night followed day. She wouldn't be able to resist her handsome hero. Antonio would be slipping a wedding ring on her finger in no time flat, and walking away as the CEO of Fortune Productions.

And Evelyn would be there, waiting in the wings, waiting for just the right moment to let the beautiful bride know exactly why her sexy Italian husband had married her.

It would be *after* the wedding, of course. No way would she be telling Paige before the big event. Evelyn wanted Antonio to get what he deserved before she set her cat among the pigeons. He was one of *her* kind, was Antonio. Born poor, and having to struggle to get somewhere in life, having to work hard and put up with bastards like Conrad blackmailing him.

Not like Madam Muck, who'd been born with everything. Looks. Money. Sex appeal.

But none of that was going to bring the bitch any happiness. Oh, what pleasure she would savour at the look in those big blue eyes once Paige knew the truth! It would be almost as good as the day she'd come home from boarding school and found out that mongrel dog was dead.

Evelyn wasn't concerned for her own fate after she'd dropped her bombshell. She was getting tired of being at the beck and call of people she despised. She'd squirrelled away a nice little nest-egg over the years she'd been at Fortune Hall. She didn't need Conrad and his money any more.

Oh, yes...her day would come. And when it did, her satisfaction would last for a long, long time.

Evelyn's presence in the room woke Paige with a jolt, her eyes flying open to find the woman glaring down at her with so much hatred a shudder of terror ran all through Paige.

'Oh!' she cried out, before she could gather herself. But once she did Paige hid her involuntary reaction behind a covering smile, pushing her hair casually back from her face as she propped herself up on one elbow.

'You startled me, Evelyn,' she said, determined never to give the other woman the satisfaction of seeing her rattled.

Paige was taken aback by the speed the housekeeper masked her true feelings as well, the hard gleam in her gaze giving way to a bland expression.

'Sorry,' she said. 'Just following orders about your meals. I knocked, but you didn't answer.'

Paige doubted the other woman had knocked at all. 'I could just have easily come downstairs and made my own breakfast,' she pointed out politely. 'You know I don't expect to be waited on like this.'

Evelyn's pale, thin lips tightened. 'But I don't take my orders from you, dear, do I? Your father's the boss of Fortune Hall. And he told me you were to be made to eat up.'

Her pinched lips unexpectedly loosened into the travesty of a smile. 'Can't have you getting too skinny and unappealing, can we? Italian men actually like women with a bit of meat on their bones, you know,' she added as she turned and walked from the room, this time banging the door shut after her.

Paige just lay there for a moment, trying to get a grip on her galloping heart. That crack about Italian men had been pointed and nasty, but she couldn't really know anything. The woman was just trying to get a rise out of her. And to make her feel lousy and unattractive.

But she refused to rise to the bait.

She might have lost of a couple of pounds these last few days out of stress, but she felt confident she wasn't too skinny. Antonio certainly hadn't found anything unattractive in her body last night.

Sighing, Paige lay back and thought of Antonio, her beautiful, handsome Antonio. She hoped and prayed he wasn't playing her for a fool, like Jed had.

There again, he was nothing like Jed, was he? Except superficially. Ironically, it was his superficial likenesses to Antonio which had attracted her to Jed in the first place. Jed too was tall and darkly good-looking. He was sophisticated and successful, intelligent and charming.

But, when all was said and done, he didn't have Antonio's depth. Or his honesty. Or his sense of honour.

Paige frowned. Those last two thoughts were at total odds with her doubts about Antonio, weren't they? If he were so honest and honourable, then he would not lie to get her into bed with him, would he? To be fair, she had no evidence that he had ever lied to any woman in his life, not even the ones he'd bedded and swiftly abandoned. If he said he was now interested in commitment, then he probably was, wasn't he? If he claimed he'd always been attracted to her, then he *had*!

A huge smile blossomed on Paige's face. What a silly girl she was, worrying about Antonio's intentions.

Antonio wasn't a creep. Or a conman. He was a gentleman through and through.

Maybe he wasn't in love with her…yet. But that didn't mean he wasn't open to the experience.

Optimism burst through her like a thousand firecrackers and she sat up. She would *make* him fall in love with her. She would show him that life with her by his side would be so wonderful he would wonder how he'd coped without her. By the time those ten days were up, she was going to have him begging her to stay with him. He might even ask her to marry him!

CHAPTER ELEVEN

ANTONIO had barely brought the Jag to a halt outside the high security wall which hid Fortune Hall from the main road when Paige came running through a side gate, dressed in blue jeans and a black jacket, a large colourful sports bag clutched in her right hand and a roomy black handbag slung over her left shoulder.

His stomach tightened at the glorious sight of her long fair hair flying out behind her, glowing in the morning sun. Her lovely face looked young and fresh and free of make-up. But that was possibly an illusion, since the bruise on her cheek was almost invisible—no doubt the result of some clever concealer.

Still, she looked about sixteen, the image enhanced by the white shirt beneath the black jacket, a garment not dissimilar to the school blouse she'd been wearing the first day he'd seen her, getting off that train at Central.

Even then, Antonio recalled wryly, he hadn't been able to take his eyes off her. Nothing had changed, it seemed. The desires she evoked in him were just as dark, and just as distracting. What was it about her which could disarm him so, and deflect him from the mission at hand? Why did she make him feel so guilty all the time when all he was doing was giving her what she said she wanted? Great sex. And commitment.

Hell, he'd already changed his mind about divorcing her later on. Now that was *real* commitment, wasn't it? And if she wanted to have children, well, that was all right by him too. What more could she ask of a husband?

115

Antonio supposed the guilt came from that four-letter word which simply wasn't going to come into the equation.

Love.

He didn't love her, and be damned if he was going to tell her he did!

Plastering a welcoming smile on his face, he opened the car door and began to climb out.

Oh, God, he was just so gorgeous, Paige thought as Antonio climbed out from behind the wheel and walked round the front of the car, smiling at her.

Antonio didn't smile a lot. He wasn't that type of man. But when he did, and his almost forbidding seriousness was momentarily lightened, he looked even more handsome, if that were possible.

'I'll take that,' he said, and reached for her bag.

Paige mumbled a thank-you and did her best not to ogle.

For he was wearing jeans. She'd never seen him in jeans before. Never seen him looking so...accessible.

Up top, he was wearing a casual blue T-shirt beneath an equally casual navy jacket, the kind with a band around the hips and a zipper up the front. The zipper was undone and the sides flapped open as he walked, showing the broad muscles in his chest and the hip-hugging style of the jeans. His still damp hair looked extra black and glossy in the sunlight, and not slicked back as severely as usual. It looked as if he'd run an impatient hand through it instead of combing it properly. There were kinks and waves all over the place, which made her want to run her hands through it as well.

'This is pretty heavy,' Antonio commented as he

slung her bag into the boot. 'I told you you wouldn't need much.'

She flushed a little at the thought of some of the things she'd brought with her. That gold lamé dress was there, as well as that provocative little pink bikini she'd been wearing the day she'd thrown herself at Antonio. It had anchoring ties on the hips and between the breasts. With Antonio admitting his fascination for undoing ties on her, one could imagine what would happen if she dared wear it.

Paige had spent a couple of breathless hours last night fantasising over *that* little scenario!

'Oh, you know what girls are like,' she tossed back as they both climbed in the car and belted up. 'They can never make up their minds about what to wear, or what to pack. Or anything, really,' she added in a rather silly fashion.

When Antonio threw her a sharp glance, she knew she'd said the wrong thing. Lord, she must have sounded like some empty-headed twit!

'I hope you don't change your mind about being with me when we're miles up the river,' he said drily, and started up the engine.

Paige took a deep breath and set about redeeming herself. 'I won't, Antonio,' she said, in a far more serious tone, her eyes seeking out his and holding them. 'You have no idea how much I've been looking forward to seeing you again. And being with you again…'

His eyes warmed at her words. 'If you've been feeling anything like I've been feeling, my darling Paige,' he said wryly, 'then I would say I *do* have a very good idea.' His head swung back to the road and the car accelerated away from the kerb.

'Now, don't chat to me till we get through the city,

there's a good girl,' he added as he eased out into the line of cars. 'I'm not used to driving in morning traffic and I don't want anything to happen to stop us getting where we're going today. I'm already distracted enough by having you sit next to me. If you say things like you've just said, and look at me like you've just done, I'll run up the back of a truck in no time.'

Paige did as she was bid, hugging his flattering words to herself during the next twenty minutes, wallowing in the excitement and anticipation of the ten days ahead. Antonio bypassed the city centre and whizzed across the harbour via the tunnel, zooming up the other side with no time-consuming hold-ups.

Antonio was the first to speak, while the car was idling at a set of red lights around Chatswood.

'Did your father say anything to you yesterday?'

'About us, you mean?'

'Yes.'

'No. I didn't see him at all. He was gone by the time I got up in the morning, and he went out for dinner last night. This morning, I avoided going downstairs till he was gone. But I sent a fax to his office just before I snuck out to meet you.' No way had she been going to give Evelyn any letter to hand to her father. Paige didn't trust her not to steam it open.

The infernal woman had hovered all yesterday, clearly trying to work out what was going on. When she'd briefly gone out to do some shopping mid-morning, Paige had raced downstairs to her father's study, looked up Antonio's home number and given Antonio a short ring, telling him not to call her at home and ask for her, in case Evelyn answered the phone and recognised his voice. She was pleased Antonio hadn't thought her paranoid.

'What did you say in the fax?' he asked.

'That I was going away up the coast with a friend for ten days. That I would be coming back home afterwards, but only till I find a new place to live.' Going to Queensland was now out of the question. She would want to be in Sydney whenever Antonio was in town.

He shot her a sharp look. 'Is that really your plan?'

'Well…yes. You must know by now I can't stand living at home for long.' It was a bit too optimistic to think Antonio would ask her to accompany him back to Europe after only ten days.

'I see,' was all he said, and fell silent. The lights turned green and he drove on, a little more slowly than before, as though his mind was elsewhere and working overtime.

Paige wondered what he was thinking, then decided to find out. 'Don't you want me to?' she asked.

'That depends,' he said brusquely.

'On what?'

'On what kind of people you move in with, I guess. According to your father, you have a habit of always choosing male flatmates who invariably end up sharing your bedroom. On one occasion he was horrified to learn you were flatting with two men, and *both* boasted they knew you intimately.'

Paige laughed. She couldn't help it.

Antonio threw her a truly scandalised look, and Paige reluctantly decided it was time to clear the air where her past history with men were concerned. She didn't give a damn what her father thought of her. He could hardly stand in judgement of her sexual behaviour with all the mistresses he had stashed around the world.

But she didn't want Antonio believing she'd jumped into bed with every man she'd lived with, despite her having done nothing to dissuade him from this erroneous belief the other night.

But the situation had changed from that, hadn't it?

'I presume you're talking about Paul and Les?' she said.

'Don't recognise the names,' Antonio said stiffly. 'But if they're the two men you enjoyed a *ménage à trois* with, then, yes, I mean Paul and Les.'

Paige sighed. If she'd known her father was going to discuss his private investigator's findings in detail with Antonio, she'd never have let the creep get the wrong idea in the first place. But at the time she'd been so annoyed with her father she hadn't cared what *he* thought.

Clearly, Antonio carried a lot of misconceptions about her. She could only hope she could rectify some of them.

'Paul and Les were gay,' she said firmly. 'All my male flatmates over the past few years have been gay, Antonio. Gay men, I eventually learnt from hard-won experience, are nicer friends than girls, and safer than heterosexual males. If you must know, the only man I've actually lived with since leaving home is Brad. Till Jed, of course. I *was* going to live with him, but you know what happened there.'

She could feel his eyes upon her, disbelief and shock in his gaze.

'Better watch the road,' she advised drily when they began to drift towards the next lane, where a white taxi carrying two worried-looking passengers was coming alongside.

Antonio swore, but kept his eyes glued ahead after that. His knuckles, however, went white on the wheel and his shoulders bunched up. His straight black brows bunched up as well.

'Are you saying you encouraged your flatmates to lie to Lew about your relationships with them?' he growled.

'Well…yes,' she confessed. 'Sort of. I…er…always warned them Lew would be around, and told them to say whatever he wanted to hear. Paul and Les particularly enjoyed themselves, I think, pretending to be my live-in studs. Of course, they were very macho-looking guys—as are a lot of gay men. I often used them as cover when a guy was bothering me.'

Her explanation didn't entirely satisfy Antonio, judging by the lingering scowl on his face. 'So when you told me you always liked to live with your boyfriends you lied as well?'

'Actually…no, I didn't.'

'That doesn't make sense, Paige,' he said irritably. 'Not if by *boyfriend* you mean lover as well.'

'Yes, that's what I mean.'

'Oh, for pity's sake,' he exploded, the car shifting ground dangerously again when he lanced her with a savage look. 'You can't expect me to believe you've only slept with two men in your whole life, especially when one of those two was a oncer!'

'No,' she said coolly, her heart sinking at this open display of disdain and disbelief. 'I've actually slept with three. You're forgetting yourself, Antonio.'

He swore. Violently. Then fell silent once more.

'Don't you believe me?' she challenged into the highly charged atmosphere.

He shook his head frustratedly, then sighed a resigned sigh. 'I suppose I must, because I can't find a single, solitary reason for you to lie.'

'So why look for one?'

He stared grimly at the road ahead for a few seconds

before nodding up and down. 'Very well,' he decided aloud, and much to her relief. 'I won't!'

He glanced over at her, black eyes narrowed and thoughtful. 'You're a wicked little devil, do you know that? Fancy letting your father believe you lived with all those men. You worried the life out of him. Not to mention me…'

As much as she was pleased by his accepting her word, she couldn't believe that last statement! 'Oh, come now, Antonio, you never worried about me. Not really.'

'I was worried sick when you first ran away from home.'

Paige could not have been more stunned.

'I felt so lousy for hurting you the way I did. And for saying such thoughtlessly cruel things. When Lew found you, and Conrad sent me to bring you home, I happily went, hoping to have the opportunity to apologise and make things right. Admittedly, when I saw you weren't exactly suffering from a broken heart, my worries evaporated somewhat. Which reminds me. What happened between you and Brad? You never did tell anyone when you finally came home.'

'Nothing happened. We were very happy together.'

'So why did you leave him?'

'I didn't. He died.'

'Good God! How?'

'He had a surfing accident. Broke his neck.'

'And you didn't tell any of us? Not your father? Or me?'

'I didn't think either of you would care.'

'I see…' He threw her a puzzled look. 'And is that why you didn't become involved with anyone else for such a long time? Because you'd lost the love of your life?'

Paige opened her mouth to tell him the whole truth, but then closed it again. She sensed it was way too soon to tell Antonio something that heavy. He might run a mile under the burden of her unrequited love for him. Best keep things light.

'You could put it like that,' she said instead. 'But I'm well and truly over Brad's death now.'

'If you say so…' He sounded unconvinced.

'I say so,' she said, then smiled over at him.

His returning smile was slow in coming, but warm when it arrived. 'You're full of surprises, aren't you?'

'I hope so.'

'Why do you say that?'

'Because I wouldn't want to bore you. I have a feeling you're a man who's easily bored. Especially with a woman.'

'Is that so? And on what do you base that assumption?'

'On the passing parade of women in your life so far.'

'I'm not the heartless womaniser you think, Paige. The women I've had all knew the score. As I said…I don't make false promises. If you must know, I was in love once too. Not long before I came to work for your father. Lauren didn't die, but she let me down. Badly. She said she loved me, but she didn't. Frankly, I still feel pretty bitter over her betrayal.'

Paige heard the hard edge in his voice. This was something she hadn't envisaged, that Antonio had been suffering from a broken heart all these years.

The savagery of her resentment over this Lauren woman tore into her breast with a dark violence she had trouble hiding. It was as well Antonio was driving, with his eyes straight ahead, and couldn't see the fire burn momentarily in her own eyes.

'She must have been very beautiful,' she heard herself saying in a hard, flat little voice.

'She was,' he admitted curtly, then just dropped the subject.

Paige could not find the courage or the will to bring her up again. But Lauren's shadow moved into the car, drying up any further conversation and dampening Paige's earlier optimism.

It wasn't till the city was long left behind and the first glimpse of water came into view on the right that the depressive atmosphere lifted. And it was Antonio's doing.

'Nearly there now,' he announced, the brightness in his voice very welcome.

Paige responded with a blinding smile of relief. 'Tell me about this houseboat,' she urged.

'Seeing will be worth a thousand words.'

'You don't sound as though you know what to expect.'

'I do and I don't. They featured it briefly on a programme on television I saw once, but I've never actually seen one, or been on one before. Still, the man on the phone assured me ours was the latest in luxury, and easier to drive than a shopping trolley. The one I've hired is their one and only honeymoon houseboat.'

Paige's eyes rounded. 'He thinks we're on our honeymoon?'

'No. But the honeymoon houseboat is the most luxurious houseboat they own, and it's kitted out just for two. Why, would you like people to think we're on our honeymoon?'

'No. I don't like lies.'

'Neither do I. We're just lovers, then.'

'Illicit lovers,' she suggested mischievously. 'Sneaking off for a dirty ten days together.'

'Mmm. I like the sound of that,' he murmured, and gave her a look which melted every bone in her body. 'Is being provocative part of your plan not to bore me?'

'That's for me to know and you to find out.'

'I aim to find out everything there is to find out about you during the next ten days, Paige Fortune.'

'And I you, Antonio Scarlatti,' she countered, her heart going like a threshing machine.

He stared at her before switching his eyes back onto the road, and the bridge ahead. Once again, Paige was proving a vastly different person from the one he'd always imagined her to be. He'd glimpsed a hint of hidden depths the other night, but today was a real revelation!

What further shocks lay in store for him? What other preconceptions were going to be smashed?

He hadn't known that her first lover had been tragically killed; he had been taken aback by the news, then startled by the unexpected jab of jealousy which had accompanied Paige's confession that she'd been heartbroken over him all these years. Maybe that was the reason for her tears on the two occasions that she'd given herself sexually to another man. Maybe she was remembering what it had been like with the only man she'd ever really loved. Antonio conceded Brad must have been a fantastic lover to have taught her so well.

Again, this thought brought more jealousy. Or was it envy?

Envy, Antonio decided sensibly. Jealousy smacked of an emotional involvement, which simply wasn't the case. Clearly, he envied Paige the experience of making love to a person she'd loved and who'd loved her wholeheartedly in return. In hindsight, it was an experience which had eluded him. And would continue to do so, now that he was no longer capable of contributing his side of such an equation.

Not that he should be complaining. Sex with Paige had been great the other night, the greatest he'd ever had—even better than with Lauren. Frankly, Lauren had been a bit unimaginative in bed. And selfish.

Lauren...

He wished he hadn't brought the woman up in his mind. He hated thinking about her. When he did, he always felt like a failure. Antonio hated failure.

His eyes slid over to the beautiful, sexy girl sitting beside him and his resolve strengthened. He wasn't going to fail this time. He was determined to win, not only Paige's hand in marriage, but her heart as well. He was going to have it all this time. The job *and* the woman.

'You're not watching the road,' Paige chided.

'I can't help it,' came his rueful confession. 'I can't take my eyes off you.'

'Well, I suggest you do,' she pointed out drily. 'Because the turn-off to Brooklyn's coming up fast.'

Antonio swore, then expertly weaved his way over to take the turn-off, a surge of adrenalin kicking in, as well as a surge of something else.

'I hope you've brought that gold dress,' he said.

'What gold dress?'

His head whipped round to find she was laughing at him, those big blue eyes of hers dancing with devil lights.

Incredible eyes, those eyes. They could look oh, so innocent and vulnerable one moment, then oh, so sexy and knowing the next. At that moment they glittered and gleamed, taunting and teasing him with the promise of erotic delights he'd only glimpsed the other night.

He was almost grateful to dear old Brad. The man had obviously introduced her to sex with a joy and lack of inhibition which could only be praised in his absence. Even his untimely passing was a source of gratitude to Antonio, because it had kept Paige's natural sexuality bottled up for years in her grief, all the stronger now that it had been released. That idiot Waltham could have been Paige's sexual genie, but he'd been a fool. His failure had become Antonio's gain.

'Just you wait,' he told her with feigned displeasure. 'Teases get their comeuppance.'

'Promises, promises,' she said, with a toss of her gorgeous golden hair.

'No false promises from me, honey. When I say something, I mean it.'

'Really! So what form does a comeuppance take?'

'I think the word speaks for itself,' he quipped, enjoying himself enormously. 'When it comes up, you'll be the first to know!'

CHAPTER TWELVE

AN HOUR had passed after their arrival at the Marina at Brooklyn, and now they were ready to start cruising the river in the incredibly compact yet truly luxurious house-boat. Twenty minutes had been spent watching a how-to video, which had covered everything navigational and operational they might want to know, and the rest of the time had been taken in being shown through the house-boat itself, with all its fittings and fixtures, storage spaces and supplies. The controls had had to be explained, plus all the other simple yet important workings.

Finally, with their luggage aboard, and a brochure and map in Paige's hand, Antonio had started the incredibly quiet engine, and angled them safely away from the dock.

Paige could not believe the feeling of exhilaration which swept through her as they headed for open waters. Putting the map and brochure down, she went out on the front deck for a while, to admire the beauty and breadth of the river, before returning inside to where Antonio was standing at the wheel, one of those rare but truly happy smiles on his face.

'This is so much more fun than I thought it would be!' she exclaimed, combing her wind-blown hair back from her face with her fingers. 'I feel like we're going on an adventure together!'

Antonio was amazed to find he felt the same away. There again, going anywhere with Paige, he suspected, would be an adventure. She was so full of life and the unexpected. She was constantly surprising him.

The houseboat had surprised him as well. In all honesty, he hadn't expected to like it as much as he did. He'd come up with the houseboat idea on the spur of the moment, because he'd wanted to take Paige somewhere right away from everyone. He'd seen a programme on TV about cruising the Hawkesbury in various craft some time back, and been awed by the untamed majesty of the river, with its wide waterways, interesting inlets and large unspoiled surrounds.

Apparently, it hadn't changed much since the days of the early explorers, when aborigines had inhabited the caves in the rugged hills through which the river wound its leisurely way in scenic splendour. There were some houses dotted along the more habitable sections of riverbank, and the occasional restaurant and supply stop to cater for the holidaymakers, but on the whole the river remained as it had been for hundreds of years. With its proximity to Sydney another attractive facet—no plane flight necessary to get there—Antonio had filed it away in his mind as a possible idea for a relaxing holiday.

Once Paige had agreed to come, however, he'd had to set about making his proposed holiday real. He'd spent a good hour yesterday morning on the phone, negotiating. It had still cost him a small fortune, first to hire the honeymoon version, then to have the darned thing fully equipped with everything from food and wine to extra linen and towels. He'd had to offer a bonus to have it all done for him that same day.

Late last night he'd been thinking he could have taken Paige to the honeymoon suite in the most exclusive hotel in Sydney for the same price. But once he saw what he'd paid for—including Paige's reaction—he felt certain he'd done the right thing.

Her beautiful blue eyes had shone as brightly as the sky overhead, and she'd fairy gushed with delight over everything, from the weather to the river to the houseboat. *Especially* the houseboat. Antonio had been more than impressed himself, both by the furnishings and the design.

Divided into three living areas, it had a stylish sitting room up front, nautical in flavour to complement the wheel, a dining area in the middle, with rich pine cupboards and green granite tops, and a master bedroom at the back, all blue, complete with a cleverly compact *en suite* bathroom. The sky-blue quilted bed was very wide, and there were porthole windows above the built-in pine bedhead, and a massive skylight in the ceiling above. Outside, there was a sundeck up top, and decks front and back. A small dinghy was tied up at the back steps— useful, they'd been told, for rowing ashore, either for fresh supplies or maybe a picnic at any of the small coves and beaches which lined the river.

Antonio wasn't so sure about picnics, but he intended taking Paige to dinner to at least one of the excellent restaurants dotted along the river. He was looking forward to seeing her in that saucy little gold dress again.

And to seeing her *out* of it.

Such thinking sent his eyes sliding over to where Paige was standing at the viewing window, a metre or so away. She'd finally taken off that black jacket, but she'd pulled the white shirt out from her waist and it was hanging loosely over her hips, hiding her figure from his gaze.

Suddenly, he wanted her closer. Much closer.

'Come here,' he commanded softly, and took one hand off the wheel to beckon her to join him.

Paige only hesitated a second before moving into the gap he'd made between his body and the wheel, her back against his stomach and chest. His hand returned to the wheel, completing the circle his body created around her. With a contented sigh, she leant back against him, her eyes closing.

It wasn't a sexual moment for Paige—though perhaps Antonio might have thought differently. The feelings which flooded through her were ones of peace, not passion. It felt as if she'd finally come home, finally found where she belonged.

With Antonio.

'Better not relax too much,' he advised drily. 'You're supposed to be watching the waterways, as well as telling me things I'm already beginning to forget.'

'Such as what?' she murmured, her eyes half opening to glance upwards into his.

'Such as what side is port and what's starboard. And which side we were supposed to pass other craft on. You see, there's this big boat coming straight for us, and I think it's time for evasive action.'

She cried out in fright, her eyes snapping forward. There was indeed a huge yacht coming towards them, and it wasn't making any attempt to shift course. Fortunately, Paige had concentrated on that part of the video which explained the basic rules of right of way.

'Right!' she ordered. 'You must always pass on the right. And always give way to sail.'

'Aye-aye!' Antonio returned, already turning the wheel.

The yacht was finally doing the same, and they passed with plenty of room to spare.

'Congratulations,' Antonio praised, and bent to kiss the top of her head. 'You just passed your first test as first mate with flying colours.'

Ridiculous to feel so pleased. But she hadn't been on the end of much praise in her life.

'This is going to be such fun!'

'Mmm. Now that we're almost in the middle of the river, we have to make a vital decision. Should we turn left, and head up-river under the bridge? Or right, and go down-river towards Broken Bay?'

'I'll have to consult the map again,' Paige said. 'I left it over there on the coffee table. Excuse me. You'll have to let me out.'

'No, don't worry about it. I've decided to go down-river for today.' And he turned the wheel to the right.

'Why?'

'There's more water that way. And it doesn't look as crowded. I'd like to find us a nice private mooring as soon as possible and drop anchor for the afternoon. It's such a lovely day. We could have lunch, then loll round on the top deck for a while.'

Paige laughed. 'I can't imagine you lolling around anywhere.'

'I have to admit I haven't done a lot of lolling lately. Wow, now that's a tongue-twister! Still, I'm very much in need of some serious lolling. You know what they say. All work and no play makes Antonio a dull boy.'

'You? Dull? Never!'

'I have my dull moments, believe me,' he drawled. 'But now is not going to be one of them. So turn round and kiss me.'

'What?' Paige gasped.

'You heard what I said. Do as your captain tells you. Mutiny will not be tolerated. It requires the same punishment as teasing.'

Paige gulped, her peaceful, platonic pleasure giving way to passion with an astonishing speed. Her heart began to pound and a wild heat ignited deep inside her body, showing her how swiftly Antonio could change her mood from one of fun and friendship to one of wildly driven desire.

Slowly, she turned in his arms, fearful of seeming too easy, yet compelled to do whatever he wanted. Because *she* wanted it too. Instantly. Intensely.

Kiss me, he commanded. Oh, God…

Her eyes lifted at the same time as her body, widening as her lips moved closer, then squeezing tightly shut when contact was made.

She began kissing him, softly at first, then with more pressure, urging him to open his mouth, dying for the feel of his tongue.

She moaned when his lips remained firmly shut, her mouth finally lifting, her eyes fluttering open with dismay and reproach.

'I don't think this was a very wise idea,' was all he said, his own eyes narrowed and glittering.

Paige had a pretty good idea what he meant. She could *feel* it, pressing hard into her belly. Yet with her blood pounding and her head whirling she wasn't thinking about wisdom. She was wanting him far too much.

'I think perhaps you should go unpack,' he advised drily.

She didn't want to go anywhere. She wanted to stay here in his arms. But she gradually saw that that would be very cruel. It wasn't as though they could *do* anything right then and there, other than make the situation worse.

'I'll go change, shall I?' she said sensibly, but with a little sigh in her voice. 'Then see about putting something together for our lunch.' The kitchen cupboards were full of supplies, with fresh food in the gas-operated fridge.

'Good thinking,' he said crisply. 'Put a bottle of white wine in to chill as well. Oh, and hand me that map of the river before you go. I'll look for a suitable mooring.'

'Right,' she returned, just as crisply, and ducked under his arms. But as she handed him the map and hurried off Paige's main feeling was frustration. She hadn't wanted to go. She'd wanted to keep kissing him, wanted to touch him, wanted to...

Her face flushed as the thought hit, her stomach tightening as she realised Antonio could have asked her to do that, and she would have. When Jed had tried to force her head down there, she'd been so revolted she'd cried out like a banshee and flown from his bed.

It wasn't revulsion which flooded her when she thought of doing that to Antonio, but excitement.

Yet she was grateful he hadn't asked, in a way. It showed he respected her feelings, and that his interest in her wasn't solely sexual.

Paige threw her suitcase onto the high wide bed and began to unpack. When she came to the pink bikini, she didn't hesitate for long. As much as she liked Antonio feeling other things for her than sexual ones, she didn't want his taking this new respect *too* far.

Alone at the wheel, Antonio let out a long shuddering breath. What in hell had he thought he was doing, asking her to kiss him? He was in the middle of a damned river, steering a damned houseboat, hardly the best place for a romantic interlude.

Although it hadn't been romance he'd been thinking of once she'd kissed him so eagerly, had it? The moment her lips had met his, a black lust had invaded his veins with the speed of a lethal injection. Thank God he'd kept his stupid damned mouth shut, because if he hadn't all would have been lost!

Oh, he had no doubt he could have coerced Paige into ridding him of his instant and very painful erection. It had been obvious she was *very* turned on. But neither method which came to mind would have endeared him to her afterwards. There was a time and place for such selfishness, and this wasn't it. His mission over the next ten days wasn't solely sex and seduction, but the making of a real relationship.

'Remember this, Antonio?'

Her voice startled him, and the map he hadn't even begun to examine fluttered from his fingers onto the floor. Antonio knew, before he even glanced over his shoulder, that he was in trouble again. When he did, his muttered oath told it all.

Dear God, *more* bows! Two on her hips, a third between her luscious breasts, all three responsible for keeping that wretched excuse for a swimming costume from falling from her oh, so beautiful body.

Antonio had seen some provocative bikinis in his life, but this was something else. It always had been, but it seemed even more so, now that Paige's figure had matured.

Ironic that the colour was shocking pink. The colour almost matched the wild pink in its wearer's cheeks as she stood there before him in an obviously aroused state. Once again the temptation was there, to have her do things which his aching flesh craved.

'Now I know why I had trouble keeping my hands off you all those years ago,' he muttered darkly.

'Did you really?' she asked breathlessly, and actually began to walk towards him, movement doing things to those inadequately encased breasts which would have corrupted a saint.

'How can you doubt it? But let me warn you, Paige, if you keep coming over here, things will happen which we both might regret later. I can see the headlines now,' he added ruefully. ' ''Houseboat runs amok! Naked lovers found drowned in river!'' '

Her approach was halted, not by his warning, but by another houseboat suddenly passing close on their port side. A man was behind the wheel and three teenage children were sitting on the sunlit upper deck, swinging their feet against the sides and watching the world go by. They spied Antonio and Paige through the wide front viewing window and waved. One of the two boys wolf-whistled. All of them stared.

Antonio lifted his hand to wave back. Paige stood rooted to the spot, blushing wildly.

Soon they were alone again.

'Well?' he said. 'What are you going to do?' He was no longer capable of resisting, if she insisted.

'I...I think I'll go cover up with some shorts and a proper top.'

His body didn't like the idea, but his brain did. 'Sensible girl.'

'Do you *want* me to be sensible, Antonio?'

'No.'

'Good,' she said, and with a smug little smile on her flushed face she whirled and left him.

He stared after her for a moment, then laughed.

'Just you wait till we're safely stopped somewhere!' he called after her.

She popped her head back into the sitting room, but only her head. 'Can I expect my first comeuppance?'

'You can depend on it.'

'Before or after lunch?'

'Both.'

'Oooh…' Her lips pursed into a provocative little circle.

'Yes, that too.'

'What too?'

'That's for me to know and you to find out. You see, I have a feeling you're the sort of girl who's easily bored with a man. Can't have that if we're to make a commitment to each other!'

Paige was on a sexual and emotional high for the forty minutes it took Antonio to find a mooring in a nice, quiet little cove. Her body burned for him, and her emotions soared.

He wanted her, plus he wanted to make a commitment to her. Her love for Antonio no longer had to be ignored, or hidden or even controlled! Her feelings could be allowed to fly, to reach the dizzying heights which she'd always known were possible.

She was just finishing making up two lunch plates of cold meat and salad when Antonio came inside from where he'd been securing the houseboat at the mooring. He stopped and just stood there, staring at her and saying nothing, a look of dark hunger in his hot black eyes.

'What?' she said, flattered and flustered at the same time.

'Have you still got that bikini on under those shorts and top?'

'Yes. Why?'

'Care to join me for a quick dip before we eat?'

'In the river? You have to be joking! It'll be freezing at this time of year.'

'That's the idea. Cool us off a bit so we can eat first.'

'Are you that hungry?'

'Mmm.' His eyes lanced hers, then raked down her body, seemingly stripping it as he went. Every nerve-ending in Paige's body began to vibrate, every erotic zone immediately went on alert. Surely he couldn't expect her to calmly eat lunch when all she wanted was him, not food.

'Yes,' he growled at last. 'Yes, I'm that hungry.'

'Oh...' Her dismay was as sharp as her disappointment. Her eyes slid away from his, confusion in her heart.

'So forget the damned salad and take them off.'

Her eyes whipped back to his, and widened. 'What?'

'The shorts and the top,' he ordered brusquely. 'Not the bikini. *I* want the pleasure of doing that.'

'H...here?'

'Right here. And right now.'

Her shorts had an elastic waist, and were easy to remove, but she still fumbled a little as she slipped them down over her hips. Letting them drop to the floor, she stepped very carefully out of them. Even then she swayed a little, and had to grab the cupboard-edge for support. The T-shirt had to be removed over her head. She felt as if she was doing it in slow motion, her breasts strangely heavy as the action of her arms lifted them upwards, pressing them together.

It was weird, that second or two when her face and eyes were hidden from his yet her body not. She could still feel his eyes upon her, feel the heatwaves of his desire hitting her like lightning bolts. They ignited a return desire so strong that nothing would be allowed to stand in the way of its consummation this time. Not even people passing by.

By the time she tossed the top aside and stood there, watching him watching her, she was his, totally, to do with as he willed.

'God help me,' was all he said as he visually coveted her curves.

'God help *me*, don't you mean?' she countered.

'Yes,' he rasped, nodding slowly. 'Yes, I would think that might be so. Now come here,' he commanded roughly.

She walked straight into his arms, and a kiss which bore no resemblance to the one she'd given him earlier. No tentativeness. Or tenderness. Just raw savagery, plundering her mouth and every misconception she'd ever had about lovemaking. And love.

For if this was love that she was feeling for this man, then it was the most dangerous emotion in the world. So violent in its intensity, and so powerful in its potential for self-destruction. Neither experience with Antonio the other night had prepared her for this…this darkly powerful and all-consuming passion.

She began kissing him back with an oral assault as brutal as his, raking her hands up into his hair, digging her nails into his scalp. He took her hair in return, winding it round one large hand and pulling her head backwards so that her mouth burst from his, her neck and back arching away from his body. With his free hand he tugged the bow between her breasts, Paige gasping when she felt the top part, then fall right away from her body.

Their eyes met for a moment, and then he kissed her again, snaking his free arm around her waist and yanking her hard against him. Her own arms wound tightly around his neck, her naked breasts and erect nipples rubbing against his chest.

She moaned under the thrust of his tongue, and the pressure of his penis against her stomach. It was so easy to imagine how it would feel, doing to *her* what his tongue was doing to her mouth.

Before she knew it her feet had been lifted slightly off the floor and he was carrying her with him into the bedroom, her body still clasped tightly to his. But, once there, he disengaged his mouth and laid her down across the bed, where she lay in a helpless state of dazed arousal while he stripped himself, then stripped her.

Stripping her proved amazingly quick, the bows on her hips as ineffective a barrier as the one between her breasts.

Paige's heart stopped when he tugged away the scrap of pink, her face heating when he just stared down at her for what felt like ages.

'You're so beautiful,' he said at last, and with unexpectedly gentle hands began caressing her where his eyes had been.

Paige moaned softly, then bit her bottom lip. When he replaced his hands with his lips and tongue she *did* cry out...with the sharpest, sweetest pleasure she had ever known.

Yet Jed's attempt to do the same had made her feel physically sick.

Antonio's mouth made her feel nothing but beautiful and sensual and loved. Oh, yes, there was love in his lips, and love in her heart for him.

'Antonio,' she groaned, when that love began reaching for a physical release.

'Antonio, please...'

When he stopped, and drove deep into her burning, throbbing flesh, she cried out his name again. It echoed through the houseboat, and possibly across the waters. And he answered her, calling out *her* name as they came together, telling her in that shatteringly intimate moment how special she was to him, how it was *her* he wanted to make love with, not just any woman.

'Oh, Antonio,' she murmured as she hugged him to her afterwards. 'That was wonderful. You were wonderful. Just wonderful...'

CHAPTER THIRTEEN

WONDERFUL.

She was the one who was wonderful, Antonio was to think many times over the next few days. A wonderful companion. A wonderful lover. And a wonderful listener. She made him want to confide in her, to share things which up till now he'd kept hidden from others for fear of being denigrated or laughed at.

A couple of days ago he'd actually found himself telling her all about his background, right back to his birth in a small village in the south of Italy, the illegitimate son of the black sheep daughter of his family. Named Gina, his mother had been a real disgrace, running round with lots of different men from the time she was fourteen. When she'd fallen pregnant, at eighteen, she hadn't even been able to point a definite finger at any man, though most of the males for miles had run for cover. The only clue to his father was that he must have been very tall, which had rather ruled out the men in the village. Possibly a tourist, the villagers had speculated. Gina had a penchant for tall men. And short men. Fat men. Rich men. Poor men.

Ashamed by the never-ending gossip, her peasant parents had finally thrown their notorious daughter and her bastard son out of the house. The man-mad Gina had gone to Rome, where she'd tried to raise Antonio herself, but it had been hard, and she'd finally turned to prostitution to make ends meet. Antonio recalled lying in a small bed against a thin cold wall, trying not to cry as he listened to the sounds of his mother being used or beaten, or both, in the next room. In the end, one night, when he was seven, she'd been bashed to death by a drunken client.

'Oh, you poor darling!' Paige had cried out at that point in his story, and had hugged him close. 'You poor, poor darling.'

He'd hugged her back and understood, perhaps for the first time, why he'd always reacted so badly to violence against women.

He'd had no trouble telling her the rest of his childhood story after that: how his grandparents had been forced to take him in, but how they'd felt ashamed of his existence. By the time he was twelve he'd been shipped off to distant relatives in Australia. They hadn't wanted him, either, but they'd tolerated his presence and at least sent him to school, where he'd put all his energies into learning languages, something he had a natural talent for. He'd left their home as soon as possible, much to their relief, and hadn't been in contact since. His elderly grandparents, he'd found out some time back, were long dead.

Paige had expressed sadness at this as well.

'Oh, what a shame! I'm sure they would have been so proud to learn of the success you've made of your life.'

Her sympathetic listening to his pretty sordid tale had touched him. She had a soft heart, a good heart. She would make a good mother, he'd realised at that point.

He'd asked her about her own mother as well. But she didn't know much more than he did. Just that the woman had been an orphan, brought up in foster homes. When she'd died she'd left behind no known relatives.

Poverty and emotional neglect, Antonio imagined, had

probably been responsible for making Paige's mother ruthlessly ambitious. And hard. And selfish.

Paige was nothing like her, thank heavens. Nothing like her father, either, except perhaps in her intelligence and lust for life.

Lust for other things as well.

Their main activity on the houseboat so far had been making love, in just about every place and position they could, except perhaps the top deck. Paige liked a degree of privacy for her passion.

Occasionally they felt guilty, and cruised a little before dropping anchor in another perfectly private little spot. He'd started one of the novels he'd brought with him, and done the odd spot of fishing. Paige spent quite a bit of time cooking. They hadn't been ashore for dinner as yet. They hadn't wanted to. Yet it was already Monday. The days were flying by.

Still, he'd rung and booked a table for the Wednesday night, since that was her birthday. And he had some special presents which he'd bought before they left Sydney, one of which he hoped would not be premature.

But by then time would really be running out, and he would have to make his move regardless.

Had she fallen in love with him as she'd said she might?

She never used the words, but once or twice he'd caught her looking at him with that wonderfully soft, almost adoring look in her eyes, and his stomach had flipped right over. There again, she had also sometimes looked at him with eyes empty of everything but a glazed desire. Perhaps all she felt for him *was* lust.

Surely not, he decided.

'You're doing it again!'

Antonio's head lifted from the towel he was lying on

to stare, first at her slender ankles, then at her shapely calves.

'Doing what?' he asked, shading his eyes from the sun with his hand as they worked their way higher.

'Nothing!'

His head lifted some more and he grinned up at her. She was wearing a pair of those short shorts of hers. Purple. And a purple and white striped midriff top which was an invitation in itself, being so bare that if she moved her arms slightly he was given tantalising glimpses of the undersides of her always bare breasts. Just looking at her excited him these days, which was awkward when he was only wearing a swimming costume. Fortunately, he was lying face-down on the top sundeck.

'That's why I came on this jaunt, isn't it?' he asked her. 'To do nothing?'

'Not all the time. What worthwhile activities have you got planned for the rest of today?'

'Well…later this afternoon, I aim to do some serious fishing. We're running out of supplies.'

'It's only one o'clock. The fish don't bite till dusk. There's a lot of time in between now and then.'

'In that case why don't you join me down here for some serious sunbaking? Pop off those clothes of yours and get yourself an all-over tan.'

She didn't exactly blush, but she looked scandalised at the idea, which rather amused him. Was this the same girl who, only last night, had prepared him dinner wearing nothing but an apron? Not the large barbecue kind of apron, either, which would have covered most of her. A saucy little tie-round-the-waist apron, with lace around the edges, which had left her naked from the waist up and totally nude at the back, except for the bow.

She'd burned the dinner in the end.

What *was* it about bows which turned him on so?

Damn it all, he shouldn't have started thinking about that now. Things were going from bad to worse in his nether region.

He glanced up at her again, and decided suffering of this kind really was masochistic when the girl of his dreams was standing right next to him.

'What's the problem?' he asked a mite testily. 'There's no one about to see you. A bit of nudity didn't bother you last night.'

'That was different,' she returned rather primly. 'That was night-time. Besides, I don't want to have skin cancer in ten years. It's all right for you Mediterranean born and bred people. You have heaps of melanin in your skin and go this lovely dark brown colour. We fair people get freckles, and melanomas.'

'I have some sunscreen here,' he suggested, determined not to give up. 'I could rub some on your back, and all those other hard to reach places,' he added suggestively.

'*That* stuff?' she scorned. 'It's downright dangerous. Mostly coconut oil and only sun factor four, and not worth spitting on.'

'Fair enough. But it does for me, so how about rubbing some on *my* back, then? I can't really reach.'

He lay back down and waited, and waited, for some movement, or an answer. When there was nothing but silence, he glanced up at her again to find her staring down at him with a frown on her face.

'What's the matter?' he asked, puzzled by her lack of response. It wasn't like her to turn down a chance of some action. Usually, she was insatiable!

'Nothing. I…oh, all right, then,' she said, and sighed.

A strange sigh, full of an oddly weary resignation, as if she was doing something she really didn't want to do, but would do it this once, *just* for him.

Paige knew she should not do this. This was something which should remain a fantasy in her mind. This was something which might lead to trouble.

Admittedly, she'd already touched him all over in the last few days. And kissed him all over. She'd even done *that*, up to a point. But this fantasy demanded much more. It demanded total sensuality and surrender to that sensuality. It demanded skill, and daring. It demanded total commitment. And total love.

The danger lay in the unexpected, and the unknown. What if she lost control and blurted out her love for him? What if the intensity of her emotions sent Antonio running a mile? Again.

He might want commitment. But not obsession.

No, no, she should not do this. Her common sense warned her against it. She was risking everything for the sake of physical pleasure.

But common sense had never been much of a match for the feelings Antonio could evoke. In the end, the temptation to bring that ultimate fantasy to life was too strong. And she was too weak...

Now Antonio sighed. With the anticipation of pleasure. For she'd squatted down and picked up the bottle of oil, and was now pouring some in the well of her right hand. His head was resting on his hands and turned to the side, his eyes slanted open just enough to see. He could not wait for her to lean over and start rubbing it into his back.

But then she did something which surprised him.

Instead of just leaning over him from where she was, she moved round to straddle his hips, her body settling onto his buttocks, pressing him hard down against the deck, producing a mad mixture of pleasure and pain.

Oh, hell!

Grimacing, he flexed every muscle he owned and gathered himself for the moment when her hands would find his skin...

Paige gave up trying to hold back the moment she touched him. If she was going to bring this fantasy to life, she was going to do it properly.

No stranger to massage, she let her fingers operate on automatic pilot for a while, kneading the tension out of Antonio's shoulders and shoulderblades, before working her way slowly down his spine.

'God, that feels good,' Antonio groaned when she reached the small of his back. 'You could do this for a living.'

'I had a lot of practice at it once.'

'What? Where?'

'In a massage parlour.'

His head snapped up and she pushed it back down. 'Only joking. I'll tell you later. I can't talk and do this at the same time.' Which was true. The feel of his flesh under her hands, plus the anticipation of what she was about to do, was turning her on so much she could hardly think.

'I'm just going to work on your legs,' she told him, her voice sounding like treacle as she lifted herself off his buttocks to kneel between his feet.

With painstaking and highly erotic thoroughness she massaged his thighs, then behind each knee, his calves, the soles of his feet, and finally each and every toe. By the time she worked her way back up his legs again Paige was beside herself with the most heart-pounding excitement. Antonio had long been reduced to silence, though he'd flinched and whimpered a few times when she'd been doing his toes.

'Turn over,' she ordered, after shifting to kneel beside him.

His eyes cracked open just enough to meet hers. 'I don't think that's such a good idea,' he told her thickly.

'But I do,' she insisted, and his eyes opened a little more.

With a shuddering sigh, he did as he was told.

'Mmm,' was all Paige could manage as she stared down at him.

Antonio stared back up at her for long moment, then thought, What the hell! Sitting up, he slipped off his togs, tossed them aside, then lay back down.

'Be gentle with me,' he murmured, his eyes closing.

She was. She was also incredibly sensual, incredibly imaginative and incredibly skilled. At some stage she divested herself of her own clothes as well, but would not let him touch her in any way.

'This is *my* fantasy,' she growled, and pushed his eager hands away to flog with impatient idleness beside his supine body once more.

Still, as much as he was dying to touch and taste her, *watching* Paige doing as much to him, with such a dark and decadent assertiveness, evoked its own wild excitement. No power on earth could have stopped him coming, yet she didn't seem to mind. She simply continued, rearousing him once more till he was totally erect again.

When she finally straddled him, and impaled herself upon his exquisitely tormented flesh, his head was practically lifting off. He could not take his eyes off her, watching her rise and fall upon him in a state of utter abandon, her breasts glistening from where she'd rubbed herself all over his oil-slicked body.

'Paige,' he cried out in warning, when he knew he was going to come once more.

He need not have worried. Because she was already there, her mouth gasping wide, her buttocks tensing as her spasms started. He groaned under the power of her contractions, then rushed to join her, their climaxes blending in one long scream of violent sensations. Afterwards, she collapsed forwards, her hair flying out then falling in a curtain over her face and his upper body. For a few minutes their chests continued to heave together but then they grew quiet, both of them spent forces.

Antonio lay there under her still, silent self, no longer in any doubt about Paige's feelings for him. He knew lust when he saw it.

His heart sank a little at the realisation, then hardened once he accepted the inevitability of the situation. She'd loved once, with a love which had stayed with her for years. Maybe she was no more capable of love now than he was.

But that didn't mean she wouldn't agree to marry him. Who knew? Maybe she wouldn't know the difference between love and lust, as Conrad had implied. She was still only young, and relatively inexperienced in life.

So he cuddled her to him, and told her how wonderful she was. She didn't say anything back, just buried her face into his chest, shuddering a little occasionally.

At least she didn't cry any more after they made love, he thought ruefully, though she was inevitably quiet, as though the experience had momentarily shattered her.

'So,' he said softly after a while, stroking her hair away from her face and eyes. 'Are you going to tell me where you learned to massage like that?'

Her chest rose as she scooped in a deep, deep breath. 'I learned watching the physio who used to do Brad,' she confessed on a long exhale. 'One day, when he couldn't afford a massage, I offered to try. After a while, I did it for him all the time.'

Antonio's gut crunched down hard at the thought that she'd done all those other things for him as well. Any gratitude he'd once felt for dear old Brad abruptly changed to a very black, very Latin jealousy.

'Really?' he drawled, and her head lifted abruptly.

'It's not what you're thinking. My giving Brad massages had nothing to do with sex. Whenever Brad needed a massage, sex was the furthest thing from his mind.' Her eyes grew quite frantic as they searched his cynical face. 'Believe me when I tell you I have never done what I just did for any man before, Antonio. You were the first. I'd been thinking about doing it with you, and finally I plucked the courage.'

Antonio savoured her confession, wallowing in a burst of sheer male ego. She'd saved that for him. *He* was the only one to have seen her like that. And to *feel* her like that.

He could almost be generous again towards her dead love.

'Why did Brad need massages?' he asked, his voice no longer carrying that hard, cynical edge. Now he was simply curious.

Sighing with what sounded like relief, she dropped her head to his chest and he cuddled her close again.

'He had arthritis. A very serious form. He'd had it

since he was a kid. But it was getting worse. That's why he moved north, to the warmer climate.'

'I see,' Antonio said. 'So how did you two come to meet in the first place?'

'Oh, I'd known Brad for years. He used to work in a take-away food place in the pavilion on Bondi Beach. He found it hard to work full-time with his arthritis. And surfing helped his arthritis. I've always been a bit of a beach addict. Anyway, he was nice to me one summer, when I was upset about something. After that, I would spend quite a bit of time with him during school holidays. He was always so easy to talk to. And he taught me to surf.'

'Did he make any passes at you?'

'No. Never.'

'But he must have found you attractive.'

'He told me later he did.'

'And you were attracted to him back?'

She hesitated at this question, and Antonio wondered why. 'I suppose so. He was good-looking, in a blond, surfie kind of way.'

'He was a lot older than you?'

'Yes, but he looked young for his age. And he was young at heart.'

'So how long did it take you to fall in love with him after me?' he asked, a bit confused by the time angle. 'Or did you think you were in love with both of us at the same time?'

Her head snapped up again, blue eyes indignant.

'No, of course not! We were just friends back then. Look, after what happened with you that day, I ran straight to Brad to pour my silly heart out. But he was packing to go north and didn't really have time to listen. He only let me go with him because he was worried I'd do something even more stupid. I wasn't living with him in that place when you came, Antonio. I used to sleep on the sofabed. We only became lovers…later…'

Antonio was truly taken aback at this news, and wasn't quite sure what to make of it. He was beginning to feel *really* confused.

'But you *did* fall in love with him?' he said, frowning.

'Not like it was with you,' she hedged. 'Though I did learn to love him. A lot.'

'And he loved you back?'

'In his way. Brad was a man who loved people, especially women. If it hadn't been me with him, it would have been some other woman. He was a pacifist, and a free spirit. He wasn't a jealous or possessive lover. I could have left him, if I'd wanted to, and he would not have tried to stop me.'

'That hardly sounds like the passion of the century!'

'I never said it was,' she said defensively, her body language showing distress.

Antonio decided to let the subject drop. He didn't think he was ever going to understand Paige's relationship with Brad. Or her brand of love. Everyone felt love differently, he supposed. He would always need passion on a grand scale. That was just the way he was. He'd been obsessed with Lauren, and nothing less would do.

He'd often thought what Paige wanted and needed was a father figure in a man, someone older and steadier who could make her feel safe and secure. Now that he knew more about her relationship with Brad, this thinking re-emerged. If she wanted some older man to take care of her, then he could fulfil that role, couldn't he? He could be lover and father at the same time.

'While we're talking,' he said quietly, 'tell me what kind of commitment you meant when you said you wanted it.'

*   *   *

Paige's heart jumped in her chest, then began to pound. Sitting up, she reached for her top and pulled it over her head. Then she dragged her shorts back on and stood up. Only then did she look down at Antonio, who was still disturbingly nude, his olive skin still shining, a stark reminder of all she'd done to him.

'What...what kind did *you* mean?' she countered, terrified of where this conversation was going. Had she ruined everything with that horribly revealing encounter? And then those revelations about Brad? What was Antonio thinking? What was he going to say?

'The usual kind,' he said matter-of-factly. 'Friendship at first, view to marriage and children.'

'Oh!' Paige exclaimed, her heart seizing up. 'Oh, I...I didn't think—I mean...I had no idea... That...that you'd want marriage and children, that is.'

He propped himself up on one elbow, his black eyes boring up into her. 'Don't *you*?'

Paige's heart galloped off wildly as everything she'd ever dreamt about suddenly seemed possible. 'Oh, yes. Yes, I do. Very much so.'

'When?'

Her runaway heart skidded to a halt again. 'What do you mean...*when*?'

'I mean when were you looking at getting married and having children? Soon? Or just some time in the mythical future? I do realise you're only young...'

How to answer that? I'd marry you tomorrow? I'd start having your baby tonight?

This last tempestuous thought swiftly turned into the most wicked temptation. But Paige steadfastly resisted it. She would not do such a thing to her child. Her child would have a father whom she was *certain* would want and love it.

'I don't think my age has much to do with it,' she told him. 'As long as you're *sure*.'

'Sure of what?'

'Of being truly wanted. And needed.'

He frowned. 'What about truly loved?'

'That would be nice too, of course. But sometimes that comes later, rather than sooner.' Oh, dear God, she hoped she was saying the right thing here. She knew he didn't love her. He'd virtually said as much. He hadn't gotten over that Lauren woman yet.

He was clearly thinking about what she'd said, but his eyes were irritatingly unreadable. 'Like it did with Brad?' he said at last.

'Yes. Sort of…'

'Sort of,' he repeated. 'So if I said I wanted you and needed you, it would be enough for now?'

'Is that what you're saying?'

'That's what I'm saying.'

Her eyes rounded. 'Are you seriously asking me to marry you?'

'I am indeed.'

She literally sank to her knees beside him. 'Oh, my God,' she choked out.

His smile looked almost amused. 'Is that a yes or a no?'

'Yes. No. Yes…'

His smile turned wry. 'I like a woman who knows her own mind.'

'But are you sure *you* mean it?' she said, her voice still strangled with emotion.

'Paige, darling…' Reaching up, he pulled her down on the towel beside him, smoothing her hair back from her face and kissing her lightly on her stunned mouth. 'I'm mad about you. *Marry* me. *Soon*.'

'How soon?'

'As soon as it can be arranged.'

Paige thought she would burst with joy. She didn't need words of love at that moment. Sometimes words could be very empty. But she hugged the loving look in his eyes and the unwavering strength in his voice to her heart. Love would come; she was sure. She had enough for the two of them.

'And her answer is?' he prompted.

'Whatever you want, Antonio,' she said, her hand shaking slightly as it reached to touch his cheek.

'I want you to be my wife,' he returned confidently, and Paige's heart turned over.

So dreams *did* come true. Who would have believed it?

CHAPTER FOURTEEN

'HAPPY birthday, darling.' Antonio lifted his glass of champagne in celebration, not just of Paige's birthday but his own success.

He'd won! And without having to feel a heel. Paige was happy. *He* was happy. Everything had worked out much better than he could ever have hoped.

As they clinked glasses across the table he gazed into the bright blue eyes of his beautiful bride-to-be and could not recall when he'd ever felt so exhilarated. He could not wait to see the look on Conrad's face when he told him his daughter had said yes to becoming Mrs Antonio Scarlatti as soon as a proper wedding could be arranged.

No way was he going to cheat Paige of a proper wedding. That wouldn't be right. This was for keeps!

Meanwhile, he had something he had to do.

'I have something for you,' he said.

Paige seemed taken aback. 'You've bought me a birthday present?'

'But of course.' And he began fishing around in his trouser pockets, smiling at her all the while.

Paige had never seen him looking as handsome as he did tonight. Their week's cruising had relaxed the tension lines around his eyes and mouth, and tanned his already olive skin to a rich bronze. He'd stopped slicking his hair straight back and allowed its natural wave free

157

rein, giving him a dashing Latin look which she found sinfully sexy.

Tonight he was wearing cream trousers and an open-necked black silk shirt which revealed just enough dark chest hair to be tantalising. When they'd walked up the steps from the jetty which led into the restaurant half an hour earlier, all the women already seated at the elegantly set tables had simply stared, first at him with hunger, and then at her with envy.

She'd felt so proud of him, and so happy she could have burst.

'Ah, here it is,' he said, and, producing a long narrow box covered in royal blue velvet, slid it across the white linen tablecloth towards her.

Paige stared down at the gold insignia of a well-known Sydney jeweller, then frowned up at him. 'But you must have bought this before we came away?' She'd been imagining he might have picked her up some little thing from the riverside supply store they'd dropped in on that morning.

'I told you your father mentioned your birthday to me last week.'

'Yes, but I didn't expect a gift like this.'

'You know, that's a very endearing quality in a woman,' he mused. 'Not expecting gifts like this. I hope you keep that up when we're married.'

Paige pulled a face at him, then eagerly opened the box. Although it *had* to be jewellery of some sort she certainly hadn't anticipated the magnificence of the gold and diamond pendant necklace. 'My goodness!' she gasped.

'You like it?'

'Antonio, it's…it's too much. Really. It must have cost you a fortune!'

'Not quite. Why don't you put it on? It might take my mind off that bow at the back of your neck.'

Paige laughed. She was wearing the gold dress, as promised, and had mischievously put her hair up, just so that very bow would always be in view. Little did Antonio know that underneath the bow was a sneaky hook and eye. He could tug at the ties all he liked, but the dress wasn't going to come tumbling down.

'Want some help?' he offered drily as she fiddled a bit with the clasp at the back of her neck, just above the bow.

'No, thank you very much,' she retaliated swiftly. 'You stay right where you are till we're well out of public view, you wicked man.'

'Spoilsport,' he muttered.

The deep V neckline of the dress could have been made for the necklace, the main diamond in the centre of the pendant nestling into her cleavage.

'Perfect!' Antonio admired. 'Only one thing missing now.'

'Oh? What?'

'This…' And he brought out another box, this one ring-sized.

Paige could only stare.

'Aren't you going to open it?'

She just couldn't, so he did, flicking open the box with a flourish and holding it out towards her, the huge diamond sparkling under the candlelight.

'For the future Mrs Scarlatti,' he murmured softly, 'so that every man knows she's properly spoken for.'

Paige couldn't help it. Tears flooded her eyes.

Fortunately, she managed to sniffle pretty quietly, but Antonio still looked embarrassed. Or was he annoyed?

'Sorry,' she muttered, using her serviette as a hand-kerchief. 'Couldn't help it. This is just so…romantic.'

Antonio's sigh sounded relieved. 'Ah…I see. Shall we see if it fits?'

The fit was a little snug going over the knuckle, but she didn't complain. Once Antonio's ring was firmly on her finger, she wasn't about to take it off in a hurry.

'Shall we have another glass of champagne to cele-brate our engagement?' he suggested. 'What about an-other bottle? This one's almost done.'

'Oh, yes, let's,' she agreed happily. 'It's not as though we have to drive the boat anywhere tonight. Or even row back.' They had safely dropped anchor a little way out from shore earlier that afternoon, and a man from the restaurant had collected them in a small power boat. He was also going to return them afterwards. A part of the service, he'd told them, to prevent any suitably soz-zled patrons from drowning in the river after dinner.

'I'm going to get very tipsy!' Paige pronounced.

'I haven't been tipsy in years,' Antonio told her. 'Can't afford not to have a clear head when I'm doing business. And I'm always doing business,' he finished drily as he refilled Paige's glass, then ordered another bottle of champagne.

She picked up her glass and sipped while considering what Antonio had just said. 'You know, I don't know why you keep on working for my father. He's a tyrant. With your expertise and connections you could start up a production company of your own.'

'That's easy to say,' he said sharply, 'but starting up a new company in competition with those already estab-lished is fraught with more hazards than you could ever imagine. Besides, I've worked much too hard to get where I am to throw it all away now.'

'Sorry,' she said, feeling a bit chastened. 'Didn't mean to make waves. I know how hard you've worked. So where will we be living after we're married? Do you see yourself working in Europe for a long time?'

'Actually, no. I'll have to go back next week for a while, but when I come back at Christmas I'll be staying. I hope I'm not premature in mentioning this, but your father plans on retiring at the end of the year.'

'You're joking! Retiring? Father? I don't believe it!'

'I think you should. That's why I told you not to worry over our getting married. Your father needs me, Paige, to be the company's new CEO.'

'He's offered you the job?'

'We were working out the terms of the contract just last week.'

'But that's marvellous! Oh, congratulations, Antonio. You must be so pleased.'

'I am.'

'We should drink to it, don't you think?'

'I do indeed.' And they both raised their glasses.

'And now,' Antonio said after their toast, 'I think we should work out the plans for our wedding. I thought we could have it as soon as I get back, just before Christmas. Is that too soon for you? It won't give you very long to organise, only about six or seven weeks.'

Paige didn't care. All she wanted was to be Mrs Antonio Scarlatti.

'Of course,' Antonio added, 'it will have to be a church wedding. I don't believe in that other kind. I don't believe in divorce either, Paige.' And he eyed her with a wonderfully stern look.

Neither do I,' she reaffirmed happily. 'Shall we drink to a no-divorce clause in our marriage contract?'

Antonio looked startled. 'You want a marriage contract?'

'No, silly. I was just joking. But you do realise that if you marry me you'll one day be a very rich man. That's if Father doesn't cut me out of his will for marrying his right-hand man.'

Paige was gratified to see Antonio seemed truly taken aback by this. 'To be honest,' he said slowly, a dark frown gathering on his handsome face, 'I hadn't thought about that.'

His reaction worried her a little. 'It's not a *bad* thought, is it?'

He looked up at her, his beautiful black eyes troubled. 'No, no I guess not. But I would hate you to think I was marrying you for your money, because I'm not.'

'Oh, Antonio,' she said, smiling. 'Why would I think that? If you'd wanted to marry me for my money you'd have made a line for me years ago. No, my darling husband-to-be, I would never think that. Come on, let's drink to our never divorcing.'

Antonio raised his glass, but he didn't drink much then, or for the rest of the evening. He no longer felt like it. Oh, he tried to remain bright and happy for the rest of the meal, for Paige's sake, but a cloud had come over his earlier elation.

The truth was he felt like a heel again, a money-grubbing, cold-blooded heel, who had allowed himself to be blackmailed and manipulated for the sake of ambition and vengeance. Vengeance against life, and Lauren.

The trouble was he no longer gave a fig for Lauren. Paige was worth ten of her. As for life…blaming his ruthless behaviour on the circumstances of his childhood was, quite frankly, childish. Such thinking was beneath him. He was a grown man, successful because of his own hard work and basic honesty.

But where had that honesty gone to these past ten days? What would happen in the future if he allowed Conrad to think he could be bought?

Over coffee, Antonio came to a decision, and his inner mood lightened. Yes, he thought. Yes, that was what he had to do!

But he wouldn't say anything to Paige just yet. Best leave any such announcements till *after* the wedding. Best leave *Conrad* till after the wedding too, he decided. His boss could be vindictive when crossed. Hopefully, Conrad would not want to ruin his daughter's happiness by that stage. But he would have to be careful. Very damned careful.

'Didn't work,' Paige said as her empty coffee cup clattered into its saucer. 'I'm still quite drunk. You didn't drink your share of champagne, Antonio,' she said accusingly, her lovely face flushed, her eyes over-bright.

He thought he'd never seen her looking more desirable, with that naughty little gold dress barely covering her luscious body, and diamonds at her throat. 'Maybe that was my plan, to have my wicked way with you,' he drawled.

She giggled. 'Surely you've gathered you don't have to get me drunk to do that.'

Antonio laughed as he inspected the account which a waitress had discreetly placed by his elbow. Expensive, he saw. But worth every cent. He included a sizeable tip in the payment, and stood up.

'Come on, Princess Paige, let's get you back to the boat, and into bed.'

'With or without this gold dress,' she said, swaying as she rose.

He raced round to take her arm and lead her out of the restaurant, guiding her carefully down the steep stone steps, only then realising how smashed she was.

'My hero,' she murmured, and leant against him during the short ride out to the houseboat.

'I have to warn you,' she whispered to him once they were alone on the back deck. 'There's a hook and eye under the bow, and it's very tricky. Designed to fool men who want to have their wicked way with its wearer.'

'Thank you for telling me,' he returned, knowing full well that when and if he got her out of the damned dress it would only be to put her to bed. He didn't want her waking up the next morning with a hangover and no memory of his making love to her. 'But I won't be having my wicked way with you just yet,' he replied. 'I think you need a little sleep first.'

'No, no, I don't want to sleep. I'm too happy to sleep. I'll be okay soon. I'll just stay out here for a while and enjoy the fresh air and the full moon,' she insisted, disengaging herself from him to turn and grip the railing.

'But it's cold,' he argued when he saw the goosebumps spring up on her arms. 'I'll get you a jacket, okay?'

'Okay.' She smiled one of those sweetly adoring smiles at him, and he melted in a way he'd never melted with a woman before.

Shaking his head, he hurried inside to get her jacket.

'I can see everything so clearly, Antonio,' she called after him. 'There's this man out in a small boat in the middle of the river. He's probably fishing. Oh, and he's got a dog. A lovely little dog. It's standing up on the bow. And— Oh, my God! Oh, how could he? Antonio! Antonio, he just threw the dog in the river!'

Paige's screeching, plus the sound of an outboard motor, sent Antonio dropping the jacket and racing out onto the deck. Paige immediately grabbed his arm and shook it violently.

'He just threw him in!' she was screaming. 'And he left him there. Went roaring off, laughing. The poor little thing's trying to swim after him. But the man's just getting further and further away. You have to do something, Antonio!'

'But Paige, if it's a dog, it won't drown.'

'It might. It's such a long way to shore from where it is. Look at it out there. It's so small. It's…oh, my God, I can't see it any more. *Do* something, Antonio!'

He hesitated, then shrugged resignedly. 'All right,' he said. 'Calm down. All right.' And he hurried to climb down into the dinghy. But it took time to untie the rope, then to put the oars into their slots.

'I can see it again, Antonio. Oh, it looks so small, and its poor little legs are thrashing away. It's going to get tired soon, I know. And then it'll sink and it'll drown. Oh, you're taking too long, Antonio! I'd be quicker swimming to him!'

'*No!*' he screamed, watching, horrified, as she kicked off her shoes, climbed up onto the railing and dived into the inky waters.

There was no hesitation this time. No taking off any shoes, either. Antonio simply stood up and dived in after her.

She had a good head start, and a cloud suddenly drifted over the moon, plunging the river into darkness. He called out her name as he swam, but she didn't answer. He thought he heard her just ahead, but it might have been the sound of his own swimming.

As much as he tried not to panic, it began to consume him. His head whirled with horrible thoughts. She was drunk. She would drown if he didn't reach her.

He swam harder and faster. Suddenly the moon came again and he spotted her, slightly off to the right, treading water and turning in circles, searching the river, looking for that stupid bloody dog. Antonio felt sick with relief. And angry. Angry that she'd risked her life so foolishly. Didn't she know that he couldn't stand life without her now?

A few more strokes and he was pulling her into his arms, feeling renewed fury when he saw how exhausted she was.

'You are a silly, silly woman!' he panted, holding her to him. 'You could have drowned.'

'Hey, there! You folks all right? You know, you shouldn't go swimming in the river at this time of night.'

Antonio spun in the water to see a small motor boat approaching them. Standing on the bow was a small wet dog, happily shaking himself.

'It...it's him!' Paige exclaimed breathlessly, pointing at the man, not the dog. 'You...you tried to drown your dog! I *saw* you!'

The man laughed, which didn't exactly endear him to Antonio. The boat slid to a halt beside them and the man bent to take Paige's hand first, pulling her easily out of the water. He was a huge man, with a grizzly grey beard and a weathered face.

'Couldn't drown Mitzy here if I tried,' he said. 'She could swim across the English Channel and back. As you can see, she's fine. Here, I think you'd better get out of there too, young fella. Swimming in the river at midnight is not such a good idea. Especially in your clothes,' he added drily.

Antonio let the old man help him into his boat as well, thinking he wished someone would throw *him* in the river at midnight. It was bloody freezing!

'But you *threw* your dog in the river!' Paige accused, teeth chattering.

The man produced a blanket and wrapped it round both of them. 'Yeah, well, the wife can't stand me bringing the dog in the house smelling of fish, so on the way home I always make sure Mitzy has a nice little dip. At night, she's not so keen to get in, so I have to give her a little hand.'

'My fiancée almost *drowned* trying to save your dog,' Antonio muttered through clenched teeth.

The man looked taken aback. 'Really? Geez, I'm sorry, mate. Thought you were just having a midnight dip.' He looked Paige up and down, then grinned at Antonio. 'I guess I was wrong. Not too many people go swimming in a party dress and diamonds! Still, she's all right now, ain't she? And you're one lucky man, marrying a brave little lady like that.'

'Yes,' Antonio said, clasping a sodden Paige to his side under the blanket. 'Yes, I surely am.'

'I'm sorry, Antonio,' Paige whispered as Antonio tucked her tight into bed. 'I spoiled our night, didn't I?'

He'd been so quiet since the fisherman had delivered them back to the houseboat. No doubt he thought her a fool. And she was, jumping in the river like that. She'd never have done such a silly thing if she'd been sober.

Antonio sat down on the side of the bed and stroked a stray strand of hair away from her face. His expression looked so serious that Paige's stomach tightened nervously.

'I have never felt so frightened in all my life,' he told her. 'I was so worried I might lose you…'

Paige's heart turned over with relief. He wasn't angry with her. He'd been worried. Taking his hand, which was now lying on the bed, she squeezed it tightly. 'You're never going to lose me, Antonio.'

Their eyes met, and she simply had to speak her heart. 'I love you, Antonio.'

His eyes widened, and she hesitated. Maybe admitting everything would lose *him*. But she had to take the risk. She could not keep silent any longer.

'I've always loved you,' she added, tears filling her eyes. 'Don't you know that? It's always been you, never anyone else. Brad was really just my friend, not my love. And Jed…Jed was an aberration of the moment, the result of my despair after seeing you with that woman at last year's Christmas party. I could not go on, I thought, wanting you, loving you, longing for you. So I tried to make a life for myself without you…'

He had her two hands in his by this point, and his eyes were stunned and sad at the same time. 'Oh, Paige…dearest Paige…I had no idea…'

'How could you? I never told you, except that one time by the pool.'

'When I broke your heart…'

'It's mended now. And it's yours, if you want it.'

'If I want it…' He lifted her hands to his mouth and kissed their fingertips. 'I can hardly express how much I want it. How much I want *you*, darling Paige. Because I love you too.'

She sat bolt upright, the blanket falling from her bare shoulders. 'You *do*?'

'I do indeed. I can't claim I always did, because I didn't. To be honest I didn't realise the depths of my feelings for you till just now, when I thought I might lose you. I'd practised being hard-hearted about women for so long that I just didn't recognise what I felt for you as love. True love this time, my darling. Not that immature, egotistical obsession I had for Lauren. What I feel for you is so much more, because you're so much more. Why, you're the most wonderful woman I've ever known, and I can't wait to marry you and have children by you.'

His dizzying words brought a level of joy to Paige which she'd never imagined she would ever feel.

'Well, you won't have to wait long,' she told him softly.

'What do you mean?'

'I'm going to stop taking the pill after my next period so that I'll be ready to have babies as soon as we're married. Oh, Antonio, wouldn't it be romantic if we conceived a baby on our wedding night?'

'You want to start a child straight away?'

'Yes, I do.'

'What about work?'

'The only job I want for a while, Antonio, is to be your wife, and the mother of your children.'

Antonio looked down at this incredible girl he loved and thanked God for women like her. Any last, lingering bitterness over Lauren was lost in Paige's arms that night, and finally Antonio was to experience the delight of making love to someone he truly loved, and who truly loved him in return.

She cried afterwards, this time, and Antonio finally realised the truth behind her tears at other times. She'd being crying for this…his love. The thought humbled him, and made him vow that he would make it up to her for everything she'd suffered because of him.

Nothing, Antonio reaffirmed the following morning, could ever be allowed to spoil things between himself and Paige. She was everything to him.

CHAPTER FIFTEEN

PAIGE woke on her wedding day to total happiness and the most delicious feeling of excitement and anticipation. Even the weather was kind, being warm and sunny.

But it was the personal warmth which had surrounded Paige during the last couple of months which continued to surprise and delight her. She could hardly believe how nice Evelyn had been since the announcement of her engagement to Antonio. And how helpful she'd been with the wedding arrangements.

As for her father...he was just over the moon, insisting that nothing was too much trouble, or too much expense. She was to have everything her little heart desired.

The truth was, however, that the only thing her little heart desired was Antonio. How she'd missed him these past few weeks! Phone calls were all very well, but nothing could compare with the real thing.

She could not wait to see Antonio again today. He'd flown in from London early yesterday morning, having had to work right up to the last minute to have everything tied up to his satisfaction before handing his job over to his second in command. He'd offered to come over straight away from the flight—he'd called her from the company car—but she'd been able to hear the exhaustion in his voice, so she'd told him to go home to bed for the day instead, and rest up for the wedding the following day. She would see him at the church, right on the dot of three. She'd promised faithfully not to be late.

They were to be married in the local Catholic Church, followed by a reception here at Fortune Hall. She'd tried to keep things small, but her father had insisted on giving her a big bash and inviting all his business cronies. She'd let him have his way, overcome by how sweet he was being to her. Perhaps he loved her after all!

Antonio had drawn the line, however, when she'd told him one night that her father wanted to buy them a house. He'd said he would buy his own house, thank you very much. He'd already auctioned the penthouse, and moved his furniture into storage. Several estate agencies were busy on the look-out for a house which fulfilled Paige's wish list.

Something not too large; she didn't want live-in staff. It was to be near the ocean, and with a large, enclosed yard which could keep children and a dog safe.

'Whatever you want, Paige,' Antonio had promised. 'Even the dog.'

A knock on the door interrupted her happy thoughts. 'Yes? Who is it?'

'Evelyn here, dear. I've brought you a special wedding breakfast. Can I come in?'

'You surely can. It's time I was up and about.'

Evelyn entered with a bright smile. 'Well, the big day is finally here!'

Paige smiled back as she bounced out of bed. 'I could hardly sleep for excitement,' she confessed.

'Same here, dear. Same here.'

Paige wasn't late for the wedding, but she was so nervous she could hardly remember a thing afterwards, except for how handsome Antonio looked in a dinner suit.

Her own appearance produced much oohs and aahs from the guests, though in reality her wedding dress was quite simple, with a fitted lace bodice, a full tulle skirt, and a matching tulle and lace veil. No trains. Nothing too fussy.

Her one bridesmaid—dressed in a cerise silk suit— was an old boarding school friend she'd kept in touch with, though not often. Antonio's best man was a fellow executive in the company, a nice enough man but a stranger to Paige. Having to scrape together a wedding party—even one so small—had been a telling indictment of their lives so far.

'The first thing we have to do once we're settled in our new house,' she told Antonio in the car on the way back from the church, 'is to start making some real friends of our own.'

He smiled and patted her hand. 'Don't worry, you'll have plenty of opportunity to do that.'

'How's that? I'll be at home, having babies.'

'Not all the time. An intelligent girl like you needs more than babies to stop you from being bored. I have a job proposition to put to you.'

'Really? What?' she asked excitedly, because in all honesty she'd been a bit worried about her impulsively romantic offer to give up work and stay home all the time. She was a people person. That was why she'd enjoyed waitressing and serving drinks, and even sitting at a reception desk.

'I'll tell you tonight.'

'Why not now?'

'I have to speak to your father first. And I don't want to speak to him till after the reception is well and truly over.'

'Is it something to do with Fortune Productions?'

'Yes.'

'Oh, goodie, I've always wanted to work there.'

He shot her a sharp look. 'Why's that?'

'Why not? I'll have you know I have some very good ideas for some new programmes. I believe I have my finger on the pulse of what people want to watch these days. Much more than Father has!'

'Mmm. I'm glad to hear that, darling.' And he leant over to kiss her on the cheek. 'We'll discuss your ideas at length tonight.'

'What? I'm not going to let you spend my wedding night talking business! You're going to be busy making babies.'

She just loved his look of mock disappointment. 'Must I?'

'You must! I positively insist!'

'Oh, well…'

They arrived at their reception, laughing.

Evelyn watched their joyous arrival, the feeling of pleasurable anticipation already building. She managed to control herself till the reception was drawing to an end and she saw Antonio leave his bride's side to speak to her father, both men leaving the room to go to Conrad's study. Clearly, Antonio was about to collect his contract. The deal was done, and about to be delivered!

Evelyn eavesdropped as a smiling Paige made her excuses as well, telling her bridesmaid that she was going up to change into her going-away outfit.

The happy couple were supposed to be going to some swanky Sydney hotel for the night before flying out for a honeymoon in Tasmania, then returning to Fortune Hall to stay for Christmas and the New Year.

Or so they thought!

Evelyn doubted there would be any honeymoon after what she had to tell the daughter of the house. Her dark excitement grew as she walked up the stairs towards Paige's bedroom. Her car was already packed and her letter of resignation in her hand, ready to be given to Conrad on her way out.

This time she didn't bother to knock on Paige's door but walked straight in, catching the blushing bride in nothing but a G-string. With her final moment of triumph at hand, Evelyn allowed her jealousy full rein, glaring her hatred at the girl's body, which had not a hint of fat, or a single physical flaw.

How good it was to see uncertainty cloud those far too beautiful blue eyes, so bright and happy a few seconds earlier, but now harbouring just a hint of worry.

'You could have knocked, Evelyn,' Paige said, snatching up a robe and hurriedly drawing it over her near nakedness.

'I suppose I could have,' Evelyn returned smugly, and swung the door shut behind her.

Everything inside Paige froze, a chill invading the room, and herself.

'What's wrong?' she asked, but deep inside she already knew. Evelyn had been pretending to be nice to her these past few weeks. It had all been an act.

But *why*?

'There's nothing wrong,' the hateful woman said, with a malicious gleam in her mean, beady eyes. 'Everything's absolutely perfect. I couldn't have planned it better if I tried. I've always thought you were a fool,' she sneered, 'but today you were played for the most prize fool of all!'

Paige did her best not to react, not to give this ghastly

creature the satisfaction of seeing her instant inner turmoil. 'I have no idea what you're talking about,' she managed to say in a surprisingly cool voice.

'Don't you now? Well, perhaps I can enlighten you. Your husband of a few hours doesn't love you, my dear. He didn't marry you because he wanted to, but because your father blackmailed him into it.'

Paige could feel herself staring at the woman, horror in her heart. It couldn't be true. Antonio *did* love her. She knew he did.

But Evelyn seemed to know differently…

'It was the morning after you came crawling home with your face a mess. Antonio had just flown in and Conrad had Jim bring him straight here. *Marry my daughter,* Conrad said, *and I will make you CEO of Fortune Productions.* At first, even with *that* carrot dangling, it was obvious Antonio wasn't keen. After all, who wants a slut and a fool for a wife? But your father isn't one to take no for an answer. *Don't marry Paige,* he added, *and I will offer the job to Brock Masters.* Naturally Antonio understood that the American's becoming CEO over him would mean the end of his career with the company altogether, so he reluctantly agreed.'

Even in her state of deep shock, Paige's mind still managed to go back to that night, when she'd walked downstairs and discovered Antonio there with her father, drinking champagne. What was it Antonio had said? They were celebrating a future merger…

That merger, she realised with growing horror, had been their marriage!

'Conrad wanted Antonio engaged to you before he went back to Europe,' Evelyn raved on. 'When he asked how he could convince you to marry him in such a short time, your father gave him some sound advice. *Seduce the little fool,* he said. *Tell her you love her. If all else fails, get her pregnant!'*

Paige thought of their first time together, and how Antonio hadn't used a condom. Not an act of uncontrollable desire, she realised wretchedly. But one of cold-blooded deliberation.

'But he didn't have to go that far, did he?' Evelyn jeered. 'You *wanted* to believe Antonio could love a little fool like you. You *wanted* to marry your handsome hero of a husband. But it wasn't you he wanted. It was the company! He's getting his contract as CEO right this minute, in Conrad's study, signed, sealed and delivered. Some hero *he* turned out to be!'

Paige could not take her eyes off the woman's ugly mouth. Neither could she say a word in Antonio's defence. Because she could see Evelyn was speaking the truth, the most ghastly, horrible, despicable truth!

'Knowing you,' the woman scorned, 'you probably won't have the guts to even tell him you know. You'd probably rather go on abasing yourself at his feet, and in his bed. Either way, it's going to be very hard, isn't it? Living with the truth, knowing your father was forced to buy you a bridegroom just to get you off his hands! People say beauty and wealth don't bring happiness. I can finally appreciate they're right. Happiness is feeling what I'm feeling at this moment!'

Paige wasn't sure afterwards how she managed not to fall apart right then and there. Somehow, she found the courage and the pride to keep the demons at bay and face her enemy with dignity, and disdain.

'Sorry to disappoint you, Evelyn,' she said scornfully, 'but you're not telling me anything I don't already know. Antonio revealed all about his bargain with Father when we were away together. He simply had to tell me once he actually fell in love with me. I'll have you know he also offered to give up being CEO of the company, but I begged him to take the job. So unfortunately, Evelyn, your happiness is short-lived, and you've lost *your* job here for nothing. Or have you already got your resignation ready?'

When the stunned woman glanced down at an envelope she was now crushing in her hands, Paige jumped to the right conclusion. 'Would you like to give it to me?' she asked, stretching out her hand and using every ounce of will she possessed to keep it steady. 'I'll hand it to Father myself. I do so hope, however, that you're not expecting references.'

There was satisfaction in seeing the woman thrown. She actually handed the envelope over before she rallied. Though it wasn't an over-confident rally. 'I...I don't believe you! You...you didn't know till I just told you now.'

'Like I didn't know about your killing my dog all those years ago?' Paige threw at her.

The woman's mouth dropped open.

'I'm not the fool you think I am, Evelyn. Yes, I wanted Antonio, and now I've married him. I don't give a damn who pushed him in my direction. Father did me a big favour, because I'm his wife now and I intend to stay that way. I suggest you get the hell out of here right now, because if you don't, Antonio will make you wish you had. You should have seen what he did to the man who dared to hit me once.'

Paige held her ground till the woman actually left. But the moment she was alone she sank slowly to the side of the bed, her emotions in tatters. In desperation, she tried to work out if anything she'd just said to Evelyn could possibly be true. Was there any hope Antonio *had* fallen in love with her? Or had it *all* been lies, right from the start? Was the charade going to be over now that he had what he wanted?

She was still sitting there, dazed and oddly dry-eyed, when Antonio came rushing into the room.

'Paige, come quickly! Your father! He's ill.'

She stayed where she was, and just stared up at him.

He frowned back. 'Didn't you hear what I said? It's your father. He's having a heart attack, I think. He collapsed, complaining of pains in his chest. I've called an ambulance and Jim is with him, ready to give CPR if needed. What on earth's wrong with you, Paige? Why are you sitting there staring at me like that? Are you in shock? Oh, God, I suppose you are. I forget sometimes how sweet you are. How…soft. Should I find Evelyn and send her up to help?'

His mentioning Evelyn's name finally snapped Paige out of it. 'No,' she said brusquely. 'No point. Evelyn's left.'

'What do you mean…left?'

'She quit. She was just here. Left her letter of resignation. And now she's gone. For good.'

'Why in hell would she do that, today of all days? Oh, who cares, anyway? You *don't*, do you?' he asked, shooting her a puzzled look.

'No,' Paige returned coldly. 'No, I certainly don't. You go back to Father,' she told him. 'I'll get dressed and come down straight away.' She stood up and turned away from her husband, feeling his hesitation and his slight bewilderment. But she could not bear to look at him. Not right at that moment.

'Go on,' she said sharply over her shoulder.

And he went.

Only when he was gone did her mind turn to her father. I hope you die, you unspeakable bastard! And I hope you rot in hell!

But even as she cursed him she knew she didn't really mean it. She wanted to hate him, wanted to hate them both! But she found she could not.

The tears came then, tears of confusion and humiliation and misery. Maybe Evelyn was right. Maybe she would *not* have the guts to confront them with their dastardly deeds. Because if she did there would be no future for her, and no children.

Not Antonio's, anyway.

But how could she live with this knowledge, and this pain?

Wretchedly, she pulled on the blue silk dress which she'd been going to wear to start her honeymoon, and carried her despair downstairs.

The ambulance had arrived and taken her father away before she could get to him. Antonio was waiting for her in the foyer, looking anxious. 'Are you all right, darling?' he asked as he took her arm and steered her through the already open front door. 'You look very pale. But the news is not too bad. The paramedic said it's probably only an angina attack.'

Jim was waiting at the bottom of the steps with the company limousine to follow the ambulance to the hospital.

'I had no idea he had a heart condition,' Antonio muttered as he helped Paige into the back seat, then joined her.

'But he didn't!' she protested. 'Did he?'

'Apparently so. He was advised to have a bypass, but he said he hated hospitals. And operations. That's why he was retiring. To take it easy. If he'd only told me the truth I would have done things differently.'

'What…what do you mean?'

His eyes carried worry as he looked at her. 'I hope this doesn't upset you, Paige, but I…I resigned from Fortune Productions today.'

'What?' Jim squawked from behind the wheel. 'Hell, Tone, you're the only decent guy in that damned company. What did you want to do that for?'

'Had to, Jim,' he said, and settled a searching gaze on his bride. 'I wanted to be my own man. Make my own life, with my new wife by my side. The woman I love more than anything else in the world. I couldn't do it working for her father, could I? People would have called any promotion I received nepotism of the worst kind. They would have lost respect for me. Respect is very important to Italians, you know. And to a husband,' he added, taking Paige's hands in his. 'I would never want to do anything to lose my wife's respect.'

Paige gulped. Oh, God, she was going to cry. All those things she'd said to Evelyn; all those made-up mad defences…they were true! Antonio might have been pushed into pursuing her, but once he had he'd really fallen in love with her. His love was so great, in fact, that he was prepared to give up what he'd worked for all his life!

Moved beyond belief, she searched for the right response.

What to do? Tell him she knew the truth?

No, no, she couldn't do that. He would believe it belittled him in her eyes. He would not be able to stand that. She had to keep it a secret, had to pretend she'd never been told.

'I think,' she said shakily, her eyes shimmering, 'that resigning was the right thing.'

'But I upset your father terribly.'

'Lots of things upset my father,' she said, still unwilling to forgive *his* part, no matter how it had turned out. 'He'll get over it. And he'll get well. You couldn't kill my father with a bus.'

'I know you probably won't believe this,' Antonio said, 'but your father loves you, Paige. I didn't believe it myself till just now. He told me how worried he'd been about you, and how guilty he felt over being such a rotten father. He blamed himself for what he saw as your restlessness. When he found out he might die soon, he wanted nothing more than to see you settled and happy with the right man. He told me that today was one of the happiest days of his life!'

Paige didn't believe that for a moment! His happiness was not so much for her, but for getting his own way. Look what happened as soon as he didn't! He had a damned heart attack. Still, if she was never going to reveal anything about this blackmailing business, then she supposed she would have to appear to believe Antonio.

'I suppose he *does* love me in his own warped way,' she admitted, the words sticking in her throat somewhat. 'And I suppose I love him back. He's my father, after all.'

'So you forgive me?' Antonio asked, with the most heartfelt emotion in his face.

'Forgive you for what?'

'For resigning. And for upsetting your father. I only hope I haven't killed him.'

Paige gave her husband's hand a comforting squeeze. 'There's no need for *you* to feel guilty,' she said firmly. 'Father will be just fine.'

Antonio's guilt lessened once he saw the man for himself again, plus the marked improvement in his colour and condition. Paige too seemed very relieved. She might not think she loved her father all that much, but she did. The last thing Antonio wanted was to feel responsible for his death.

'You worried the life out of me,' he said by Conrad's bedside.

'I worried the life out of myself. Think I might have that operation after all.'

'Good idea,' Paige chipped in. 'Then you can stop this retiring nonsense and look after your own company.'

Conrad smiled a wry smile at his daughter. 'Just look at her. Married less than a day and already telling her old man what to do. I still can't believe the change in you, missy. You're a different person. Just shows you what the right man can do. Speaking of the right man… I know you won't change your mind, Antonio, but would you stay on as caretaker CEO, just till I'm on my feet?'

'Can't Brock Masters do that?' Antonio asked, rather tongue-in-cheek.

'Brock Masters! You have to be joking. He's already been given his third warning. Damned fool's been taking drugs. He'll be out by Christmas.'

'Best move you ever made. And, no, Conrad, I won't be staying on as acting CEO. I told you my reasons for leaving today, and you have to appreciate they're very good ones.'

Conrad nodded resignedly, then smiled at both of them. Antonio smiled back. He might be a devious old devil, and what he'd done was very wrong, but Antonio would still always be grateful to his father-in-law for bringing him a happiness beyond anything he could have hoped for.

*   *   *

Beside him, Paige was slowly coming to the same thinking herself. No matter what her father's motives, he'd given her Antonio, hadn't he? Hard to hate a man who'd made her dearest dream come true.

Later that night, she snuggled into Antonio's arms after some very serious lovemaking and asked him a very important question.

'Would you like a boy or a girl first?'

It was a question which would consume them for the next nine months, especially after the doctor confirmed that Paige had indeed conceived, either on her wedding night or soon after. Antonio could not conceal his pleasure when the ultrasound at four months revealed a baby who was decidedly male.

By the time Julius Richard Scarlatti was born the following September, his ecstatic parents had moved into a nice four-bedroomed house on Maroubra Beach, painted the nursery green in case the next child was a girl, and bought a four-year-old black mongrel from the local dog pound who'd been on death row. They'd also completed production of the first series of an hourly programme called *The Romance Show*, which showed viewers romantic places, holidays, hotels, restaurants, clothes, lingerie, gifts and books. It had been Paige's idea.

In the year it went to air, everyone who watched the show quickly became addicted to its feel-good theme. Most agreed that the most romantic aspect of the show was the producers. The way they looked at each other sometimes, when they were shown, photographed in the newspaper. The way they laughed, and held hands. They looked so obviously in love with each other. So obviously happy together.

Which they were.

VIVA LA VIDA DE AMOR!

They speak the language of passion.

In Harlequin Presents®, you'll find a special
kind of lover—full of Latin charm. Whether
he's relaxing in denims or dressed for dinner,
giving you diamonds or simply sweet dreams,
he's got spirit, style and sex appeal!

Latin Lovers is the new miniseries
from Harlequin Presents® for anyone
who enjoys hot romance!

Meet gorgeous Antonio Scarlatti in
THE BLACKMAILED BRIDEGROOM
by Miranda Lee, Harlequin Presents® #2151
available January 2001

And don't miss sexy Niccolo Dominici in
THE ITALIAN GROOM
by Jane Porter, Harlequin Presents® #2168
available March 2001!

Available wherever Harlequin books are sold.

CELEBRATE VALENTINE'S DAY WITH HARLEQUIN®'S LATEST TITLE— *Stolen Memories*

Available in trade-size format, this collector's edition contains three full-length novels by *New York Times* bestselling authors Jayne Ann Krentz and Tess Gerritsen, along with national bestselling author Stella Cameron.

TEST OF TIME by **Jayne Ann Krentz**—
He married for the best reason.... She married for the only reason.... Did they stand a chance at making the only reason the real reason to share a lifetime?

THIEF OF HEARTS by **Tess Gerritsen**—
Their distrust of each other was only as strong as their desire. And Jordan began to fear that Diana was more than just a thief of hearts.

MOONTIDE by **Stella Cameron**—
For Andrew, Greer's return is a miracle. It had broken his heart to let her go. Now fate has brought them back together. And he won't lose her again...

Make this Valentine's Day one to remember!

Look for this exciting collector's edition on sale January 2001 at your favorite retail outlet.

HARLEQUIN®
Makes any time special ™

Visit us at www.eHarlequin.com

PHSM

Lindsay Armstrong...
Helen Bianchin...
Emma Darcy...
Miranda Lee...

Some of our bestselling writers are Australians!

Look our for their novels about the Wonder from Down Under—where spirited women win the hearts of Australia's most eligible men.

THE **AUSTRALIANS**

Coming soon:

THE MARRIAGE RISK
by Emma Darcy
On sale February 2001, Harlequin Presents® #2157

And look out for:

MARRIAGE AT A PRICE
by Miranda Lee
On sale June 2001, Harlequin Presents® #2181

Available wherever Harlequin books are sold.

HARLEQUIN®
Makes any time special ™

If you enjoyed what you just read,
then we've got an offer you can't resist!

Take 2 bestselling love stories FREE!

Plus get a FREE surprise gift!

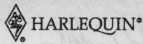

HARLEQUIN®

makes any time special—online...

eHARLEQUIN.com

your romantic life

—Romance 101—
♥ Guides to romance, dating and flirting.

—Dr. Romance—
♥ Get romance advice and tips from our expert, Dr. Romance.

—Recipes for Romance—
♥ How to plan romantic meals for you and your sweetie.

—Daily Love Dose—
♥ Tips on how to keep the romance alive every day.

—Tales from the Heart—
♥ Discuss romantic dilemmas with other members in our Tales from the Heart message board.

Tyler Brides

It happened one weekend...

Quinn and Molly Spencer are delighted to accept three bookings for their newly opened B&B, Breakfast Inn Bed, located in America's favorite hometown, Tyler, Wisconsin.

But Gina Santori is anything but thrilled to discover her best friend has tricked her into sharing a room with the man who broke her heart eight years ago....

And Delia Mayhew can hardly believe that she's gotten herself locked in the Breakfast Inn Bed basement with the sexiest man in America.

Then there's Rebecca Salter. She's turned up at the Inn in her wedding gown. Minus her groom.

Come home to Tyler for three delightful novellas by three of your favorite authors: Kristine Rolofson, Heather MacAllister and Jacqueline Diamond.

HARLEQUIN®
Makes any time special™

MAITLAND MATERNITY

Where the luckiest babies are born!

In February 2001, look for

FORMULA: FATHER

by Karen Hughes

Bonnie Taylor's biological clock is ticking!

Wary of empty promises and ever finding true love,
the supermodel looks to Mitchell Maitland, the clinic's
fertility specialist, for help in becoming a mother. How can
Mitchell convince Bonnie that behind his lab coats and
test tubes, he is really the perfect man to share her life
and father her children?

*Each book tells a different story about the
world-renowned Maitland Maternity Clinic—
where romances are born, secrets are revealed...
and bundles of joy are delivered.*

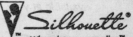

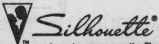